PENGUIN

UNSAID: AN ASIAN ANTHOLOGY

Anitha Devi Pillai (PhD) has authored and edited creative and non-creative fiction books as well as translated a historical fiction novel, *Sembawang: A Novel* (2020) from Tamil into English, which was shortlisted for the Singapore History Prize, awarded by the National University of Singapore and the Best Literary Book Award by the Singapore Book Publishers Association. She also loves writing poetry. Some of her poems have made their way into the classrooms in Singapore, India, Australia and the Philippines. Many of her work explore themes such as identity, heritage and culture.

She is best known for her research into the Singapore Malayalee community that was supported by a National Heritage Board (Singapore) grant and resulted in the publication of *From Kerala to Singapore: Voices from the Singapore Malayalee Community* (2017). For this study, Anitha was awarded the Pravasi Express Research Excellence Award in 2017.

Her other books are *Project Work: Exploring Processes, Practices and Strategies* (2008), *From Estate to Embassy: Memories of an Ambassador* (2019), *A View of Stars: Stories of Love* (2020), *A Tapestry of Colours 1: Stories from Asia* (2021), *A Tapestry of Colours 2: Stories from Asia* (2021) and *The Story of Onam* (2021).

Anitha's favourite genres to write and teach are the short story and creative non-fiction prose. Her stories have appeared in various anthologies including *The Best Asian Short Stories 2019*, *Letter to my Son* (2020) and *Food Republic:*

A Singapore Literary Banquet (2020). She is currently working on a collection of short stories focusing on food and love.

She is the co-director of the *16th International Conference on the Short Story in English* and editor for the prose (fiction and creative non-fiction) section of the *Practice, Research and Tangential Activities (PR&TA)* literary journal.

In a parallel life, she is an applied linguist and teacher educator at the National Institute of Education (NIE), Nanyang Technological University (NTU), Singapore where she teaches courses on various forms of writing and trains English language teachers to teach writing. Anitha is a three-time recipient of teaching awards: Excellence in Teaching Commendation Award from NIE, NTU in 2018 and the SUSS Teaching Merit Award in 2013 and 2014 from the Singapore University of Social Sciences.

CONTRIBUTORS

Saras Manickam is a Malaysian short story writer. Her stories have appeared in Malaysian anthologies such as *Silverfish New Writing* (2006 and 2008); and *Readings from Readings* (2011 and 2012). In 2017, her story, 'Charan' won the DK Dutt Memorial Award for Literary Excellence. In 2019, her story, 'My Mother Pattu' won the regional prize for Asia in the Commonwealth Short Story Contest.

Cherrie Sing is a Filipino-Chinese writer born in Manila, Philippines. She holds two degrees: Literature and Finance from De La Salle University. She was also a writing fellow in two national workshops in the Philippines, the prestigious Silliman National Writers' Workshop and Iligan Writers' Workshop. Some of her poems and short stories have been published in national magazines like *Panorama*, *Philippine Graphic* and *The Mirror*. Outside the country, one of her poems was included in the Hong Kong e-corpus poetry for children, and another story was published in Malaysia's *Twenty-Two Asian Stories* in 2016. Her works mostly deal with the Filipino-Chinese identity in the Philippines. She is proudly not affiliated with any academic institutions but works in the private transportation industry.

Paul GnanaSelvam is an Ipoh-born writer and poet whose work often focuses on the experiences, issues and identity conflicts of those in the Indian diaspora. Writing since 2006, he has published both locally and internationally in anthologies, literary journals and e-magazines. His first collection of short stories *Latha's Christmas and Other Stories* was published in 2013, while *The Elephant Trophy and Other Stories* was published by Penguin-Random House, SEA in 2021. He currently teaches writing while undertaking research focusing on instructional communication and L2 writing in higher education.

Adwiti Subba Haffner is a poet, short-story writer and a transformational coach who has published two books, *101 Motivational Tips for your Success* (2013) and *Abundance is Yours* (2013) which was ranked first in the spiritual section of books on Amazon. Her poem, 'Tonight, let me not cry', was awarded the first prize in the Alabama State Poetry Society Competition in 2017. In 2018, her poems, 'When Green Apples Speak' and 'The Bluebruisepurple Shades of Metoo' were awarded the third prize in two competitions. In 2022, her poems, 'Salt has Reached My Lips' was awarded third prize and 'I Ask the Sea' was awarded second prize in the Alabama State Poetry Society competition.

Niduparas Erlang was born in Serang in 1986. He writes stories, novels, essays and articles in journalism. His latest novel, *Burung Kayu* (Wooden Bird) (2020), received special jury recognition in the 2019 Jakarta Arts Council Novel Competition and won the prestigious Khatulistiwa Literary Award in 2020. His other books include the short story collections *La Rangku* (The Kite Prince) (2011). He was the winner of the 2011 Surabaya Arts Festival Short Story Manuscript Competition, *Penanggung Tiga Butir Lada Hitam di Dalam Pusar* (The One with Three Peppercorns in His Bellybutton) (2015), the winner of the 2015 Siwa Nataraja Short Story Manuscript Award and has produced a 2017 volume which includes both collections. He currently runs the Aing Community, facilitates the interdisciplinary cultural heritage and arts centre Banten Girang Laboratorium and helps to manage the Multatuli Art Festival. He received his Master's in Cultural Studies with an Oral Traditions specialization from Indonesia University and is an Indonesian literature professor at Pamulang University.

Annie Tucker is a Los Angeles-based writer, researcher and translator from Indonesian. She holds a PhD in Culture and Performance from the University of California, Los Angeles. Her translation of Eka Kurniawan's *Beauty is a Wound* was a *New York Times* notable book and won the 2016 World Reader's Award.

Dennis Yeo lectures at the English Language and Literature Academic Group at the National Institute of Education, Nanyang Technological University. He has taught at primary, secondary and junior college levels in a career spanning three decades and was subject head (Literature), head of department

(Pastoral Care and Career Guidance) and vice-principal at Pioneer Junior College.

A few of his poems have found their way into anthologies like *Love at the Gallery* (2017), *A Luxury We Must Afford* (2016) and *This is not a Safety Barrier* (2016). His first short story 'Close to You' can be found in *A View of Stars: Stories of Love*. His father was from Segamat and he did lose a baby tooth biting into a turtle made of peanut brittle.

S.P. Singh is a retired army colonel who is an alumnus of the prestigious National Defence Academy, Khadakwasla, Pune, and Indian Military Academy, Dehradun. The officer is a voracious reader and a painter. His debut novel, *Parrot under the Pine Tree*, published in May 2017, was shortlisted for the Best Fiction Award at the Gurgaon Literary Festival 2018 and was nominated at the Valley of Words Literary Festival 2018.

Gaurav Bajpai grew up in Kanpur, the city on the banks of the holy Ganges. Stories became a part of his daily life, whether they were at a temple near the riverbanks or from his mother. Fascinated by those tales, he wrote some and was encouraged by his friends and family. A finance professional, he travelled extensively, discovering and meeting exciting people and being a part of their life and stories. Finally, he moved back to India in 2019 from New Jersey and took to writing full-time to get these experiences on paper. He recently published his first book, *Folktales of Faujpur*, a collection of eleven urban short stories.

He resides in Gurgaon, India, with his wife and a six-year-old daughter. When he is not writing, he goes on food adventures to try various cuisines and spends time with his daughter, making a birdhouse or taking a bike ride in the neighbourhood.

Adriana Nordin Manan juggles eight professional roles: writer, playwright, translator, researcher, curator, dramaturg, educator and entrepreneur. Born, raised and based in Kuala Lumpur (KL), she is fascinated by the expanse of stories as mirrors to society and monuments to the human condition. In 2019, her translation of *Pengap* by Lokman Hakim was shortlisted for The Commonwealth Short Story Prize, a first for Malay language submissions in the history of the prize. Adriana's work has been published in *adda*, the literary magazine run by Commonwealth Writers, and *Lost in Putrajaya*, an anthology by Fixi, an independent publishing house in KL. Adriana is currently completing her debut, full-length play, which grapples with issues of diaspora, cultural psyche and belonging. She speaks Malay, English and Spanish.

Razia Sultana Khan earned her MA in Linguistics from the University of York (UK) and her PhD in Creative Writing from the University of Nebraska-Lincoln (USA). Her short story 'Alms' was published in *Best New American Voices*, 2008, (Ed. Bausch, Harcourt Publishers). Her other stories have appeared in *A Rainbow Feast: New Asian Short Stories* (Malaysia: Marshall Cavendish, 2010), *Twenty-two Asian Short Stories* (Silverfish, Malaysia, 2016) and *The Best Asian Short Stories 2019* (Ed. Bustani, Kitaab Singapore). She frequently writes for local journals and newspapers. She has taught at various public and private universities in Bangladesh. In addition to writing, her passion is oil painting. Her first solo art exhibition was held in Dhaka, in February 2020. She is immensely proud of her Chinese snuff-bottle collection of the Qing dynasty. She lives in Dhaka with her two turtles.

Danton Remoto's novel, *Riverrun*, was published by Penguin Random House in 2020. Bookriot.com, the largest independent publishing platform in the US, called his novel 'one of the five most anticipated books by an Asian author for 2020'. He was a professor of creative writing and head of school-English at the University of Nottingham, Malaysia. He has published a book of short fiction, three books of poems and five non-fiction books which were all written in English. He was a fellow at the Cambridge Seminar on Contemporary Writing at Downing College, the Bread Loaf Writers' Conference in Vermont and the MacDowell Artists' Residency. He studied at Ateneo de Manila University, Rutgers University, University of Stirling and the University of the Philippines. His body of work is listed in *The Routledge Concise History of Southeast Asian Writing in English*, *The Oxford Research Encyclopedia of Literature*, and *The Encyclopedia of Postcolonial Literature*. His next novel is a supernatural tale, and his website is www.dantonremoto.com.

William Quill (pen name) was born in Los Angeles, California. He primarily writes short stories and poems, combining history and fantastical elements while exploring universal themes. William published *Seven Points* (2020), a collection of dystopian short stories, and is currently working on *Dictemotum*, a collection of poems, to be published in late 2022. He is a historian by training and publishes his research under his name Samuel Boucher.

Keith Jardim is from Port of Spain, Trinidad, and a graduate of Emerson College, Boston, where he earned a Merit Fellowship for his MFA (Master of Fine Arts). Jardim's PhD is from the University of Houston's Creative Writing and English Literature programmes. He has won The Paul Bowles Fiction Award, a James Michener Fellowship, and a C. Glenn Cambor Fellowship. He has also been shortlisted for *American Short Fiction*'s contest and *Glimmer Train*'s Open Fiction Contest among other honours. His stories and essays have appeared in *Denver Quarterly*, *Wasafiri*, *The Guyana Arts Journal*, *Moving World*s, *Mississippi Review*, *Atlanta Review*, *Short Story*, *Caribbean Quarterly*, *The Haunted Tropics: Caribbean Ghost Stories*, *Trinidad Noir*, *The Antigonish Review* and elsewhere. His first book, *Near Open Water: Stories* was a semi-finalist for the 2012 OCM Bocas Prize for Caribbean Literature; later that year, it was included on *World Literature Today*'s Nota Bene List. He was a senior lecturer in English and creative writing at University of Malaya, Malaysia (2020–22).

Ismim Putera is a poet and writer from Sarawak, Malaysian Borneo. He is the author of a poetry chapbook, *Tide of Time* (Mug and Paper Publishing, 2021), and recently won the third place in the 7th Singapore Poetry Contest. His latest works can be found in *Anak Sastra*, *Prismatica Magazine* and *Be Me: LGBTQ+ Stories of Belongings*.

Clara Mok loves reminiscing about her childhood and wishes to capture snippets of Singapore's past before they disappear. For 'The Lantern Maker's Wife', she interviewed Mr Lim Choon Kiang, 93, a hobbyist lantern maker, who has been making lanterns by hand for his family for over 30 years.

He made an Angry Bird cellophane lantern for her and she cherishes it dearly. She is thankful to Ms Mary Tan for inviting her to her family's traditional Mid-Autumn Festival celebrations.

Clara graduated from Nanyang Technological University, Singapore. She was selected for the Mentor Access Project 2016–17 by the National Arts Council, Singapore. 'The Lantern Maker's Wife' was developed under Ms Josephine Chia's mentorship. Her short stories were published in *Singapore at Home: Life Across Lines* and *A Tapestry of Colours 1 and 2*. She is an English educator and shares her love for writing with her students.

Unsaid: An Asian Anthology

Edited by Anitha Devi Pillai

PENGUIN BOOKS
An imprint of Penguin Random House

PENGUIN BOOKS

USA | Canada | UK | Ireland | Australia
New Zealand | India | South Africa | China | Southeast Asia

Penguin Books is part of the Penguin Random House group of companies
whose addresses can be found at global.penguinrandomhouse.com

Published by Penguin Random House SEA Pte Ltd
9, Changi South Street 3, Level 08-01,
Singapore 486361

Penguin
Random House
SEA

First published in Penguin Books by Penguin Random House SEA 2022
Anthology copyright © Anitha Devi Pillai 2022
Copyright for individual articles vests with respective Authors.

ISBN 9789815017090

Typeset in Garamond by MAP Systems, Bangalore, India

www.penguin.sg

Contents

Editor's Note

Some stories come from you, and yet others find you.

UNSAID: An Asian Anthology is a collection of short stories that landed on my lap as I was working on a different project. And as one story after another started coming into my path, it became increasingly clear that they belonged together.

The stories were all intriguing and enticing with just a tinge of mystic and shadows. There were stories about othering, about complicated and knotted relationships at home and in the society, and the dark and unknown that live amongst us. Collectively, they captured some of the greyest areas the hearts and the souls of man – in various parts of Asia.

This book would not have been possible without the short story writers and contributors to this anthology; Sumi Thomas for her able assistance; and Nora Nazerene, Publisher, Penguin Random House SEA Pte Ltd, for her faith in the collection of stories and writers. This book would not have been possible without all their collective support.

I hope that what is left unsaid amongst the pages of this anthology will have you thinking about it for a long while—even after you finish reading the book.

Anitha Devi Pillai

The Others

When We Are Young

Saras Manickam

When I got up this morning and unmuted the phone, I knew there would be a couple of missed calls from Hsian and Arun. There were seven: two from Arun from yesterday evening and five from Hsian. I wasn't in any mood to call back. *Die, Arun. Die. Die.* He'd probably wanted to blether an apology while Hsian—well, he was always playing peacemaker between Arun and me, what else was new?

'We've been friends for too long, come on, Farida,' he'd say.

And I'd say, 'Friends? He's no friend, Hsian, not any longer. What kind of friend calls you those dreadful ugly names?'

More than anger was Arun's treachery. It ate into me, a parasite tunnelling into my brain. Arun had always been more than a neighbour; he'd been my brother, far more than my own. And I'd thought he'd felt the same way about me. Yesterday though, all friendships had come undone, ripped and shredded until I thought I'd die from the pain, the pain. *Die, Arun, die.*

Hsian rang again twice—I ignored the calls—while I was having breakfast with Abah. Just the two of us, the way I liked. My mother and Kak Minah were in the kitchen discussing lunch. My brother, Zul, didn't believe in early breakfasts on weekends. He was still in his room. I could hear him make waking-up sounds. He was something else, that boy; yesterday evening, he was suddenly all subdued, all stricken. He'd come home after a rough game of football, with his jersey bloodied and torn. He went to bed without his dinner. Then, when I came down to the kitchen for a drink in the middle of the night, I found him burning his jersey at the sink. I mean who destroys an original Man U jersey? He looked at me and shook his head. *Okay, okay, no questions.* I had my problems, he had his.

My phone rang again. 'Answer the phone,' Abah said. It was Hsian, still playing peacemaker. I geared myself to do battle.

'Don't talk to me about Arun, Hsian,' I snapped by way of 'hello'. 'He's dead to me, understand?' Except Hsian began sobbing.

'We're in the hospital. Arun . . . Arun is . . .' He broke down and I found myself screaming: 'Arun? Hsian! ARUN!'

My father took the phone from my hand and found out what had happened. I must have shrieked so loudly that Mak and Kak Minah came running from the kitchen. Even Zul rushed out of his room. Anyways, coming back, Abah said Arun was in the hospital and he'd drive me here. No questions, just a statement: 'He's alive, Farida.' That's my Abah.

Mak did try to stop us. 'Hold on, she can't go. She's got no business at the hospital. She's not family.'

Kak Minah fixed her with a beady look. 'As far as I know, right from kindergarten, this girl has been going straight to

Arun's house after school. She eats there, does her homework there, spends all her time there, coming back here just to bathe, pray and sleep.' Her face was grim. 'She's family all right, believe me.' Kak Minah, our maid, was the de facto ruler of our household. My mother knew that if we didn't please her, she'd leave us and return to Indonesia.

In the car, Abah asked in his soft voice, 'What happened between you and Arun, Farida?'

'I don't want to talk about it,' I said, before blurting out, 'We quarrelled. He got an offer from the university.'

'Engineering?'

'No.' My voice was low. 'Consumer Studies.'

'Consumer what?' Abah looked at me. 'He scored 3As in his *STPM* and gets Consumer whatsit. Hell. You scored 3As in your A-levels and you got dentistry in Australia on a full scholarship.' He gave a little bark. 'The perks of being the right race in this country.'

Not my Abah too. I closed my eyes.

* * *

So here I am in the hospital, trying to block out the smell of disease that hovers in the air, not quite masked by strong antiseptics. It's not the cheeriest of places. I'm looking at Arun. Head injuries. Broken ribs. I hope he burns in hell, whoever did this to my friend. Tubes link his bandaged chest, arm, finger to drips and machines. I feel a rush of tenderness and it takes me by surprise.

'I mean, dude,' I tell him silently, 'all these years, if I ever wasted brain space on you, it was because you were my *macha* next door. Of course, I also thought of that *monyet*, Hsian who is now blubbering next to you. Okay, okay, I admit I spent far more time thinking of him than you. In my soppiest moments I've even doodled, *Farida heart Hsian. Heart. Heart.* Yesterday morning—was it only yesterday?—I never ever wanted to lay eyes on you again, and now, look—' a sob escapes from my throat, 'I'm at your side, crying and all astonished that I'm crying, macha!' My face aches with the unaccustomed crying.

I turn to look at Auntie Ruku and Hsian, their hands gentle on Arun's body as if their touch with the weight of all their love would surely bring him back from the brink. More than anything I want to run to them, feel the warmth of Auntie Ruku's embrace, but I hold back. Instead, I turn to Arun again and continue my silent conversation with him.

'Hey, Arun, guess what? I met some of your "well-wishers" outside the ward by the way. They were muttering: "Why is she here, that Melayu girl? His girlfriend, ah? Cannot get any Indian girl? I hear the Malays beat him up. All useless. Drug addicts. Not enough the Malays did this to him, he's got a Malay girl and she wants him to convert, izzit? And that Cheenen? What's he doing here? No Indian friend, ah?"

'I turned to them, not caring if my words cut like a razor. "Not girlfriend. *Kawan, lah.* Geddit?" They wouldn't. No matter. Adults are all idiots, including this lot, and anyways, I'm not budging from your side. Hsian isn't either. And certainly not Auntie Ruku.'

The room is quiet except for the beep of the machines. The three of us are in separate bubbles of grief. We don't talk to each other, yet the unspoken tension crackles beneath the surface. I expect any time now for Auntie Ruku to tell me to get lost. 'Go away girl, you never wanted to see us again, remember?' During 'the quarrel', she had tried to grab my hand only for me to shake it off, as if it were infectious.

I wait. To tell the truth, I half expect Arun to open his eyes now that we're all sitting around his bed—you know *lah*, that's how it always works in the movies. Cue: sad, heartbreaking music. Camera zooms into a close-up of a beautiful young girl with wet face (me) gazing at a boy in a coma in a hospital bed. Boy's eyes flicker and slowly open. He's awake! Sad music changes to a joyful tune.

Arun's not making this easy, is he? His eyes remain stubbornly closed.

'Listen, Auntie Ruku, Farida,' Hsian speaks softly. 'Let's talk to him. I'm sure he can hear us.' Hsian has dark circles hooding his eyes. When he looks at me, he appears watchful, wary just the way Uncle Foong's dog looks, waiting for the quick, sudden kick in the belly. It bewilders me.

'What to say, Hsian?' Auntie Ruku cries. 'If anything happens to him, I will die.' Her grief has shrunken her. She avoids me. It cuts me to the quick even as I know I have only myself to blame.

'I want to say something.' I speak directly to Arun. 'About my Auntie Ruku.'

Auntie Ruku murmurs, 'No need, no need.'

'She's not my aunt. She's not of my race or my religion. She's no blood relative at all. *Calling her "Auntie" just as you do is a mere gesture of respect. You don't actually have to care for her or anything.* That's what my mother tried to drum into me. No matter. From the day I first met her, I've loved Auntie Ruku. That's what I try to tell my mother but as usual, she isn't listening to me. Well, you know my mum, I'm not exactly her favourite offspring, right?'

My battles with my mother are a regular feature. I am not pliable like my brother Zul. I am not obedient like him.

More importantly for her, I refuse to wear the tudung like she wants me to.

'I remember the first time I met you both. Our new neighbours. 1988. I was five. The kindergarten school bus screeched to a stop right in front of my house to offload the three of us. I could see Kak Minah, our maid, waiting at our gate. By the way, Arun, Kak Minah has been with us . . . like forever. She must be at least a hundred years old now.' Behind me, I heard Hsian turn a giggle into a snort. I heard Auntie Ruku shift in her chair.

'She was carrying Zul in her arms. Hovering at the sidewalk was an Indian woman in a strange dress.'

'Strange dress? That was a housecoat, girl. And it was new.'

'First to get down was the new boy who had just moved next door. He went straight to the Indian woman. I was climbing down the steps when that monyet Hsian . . .'

'Monyet? *Moi*? You *lah* the monkey!'

Finally! My heart sings. I continue. 'When that monyet Hsian pushed me aside and scampered down first. I fell. Kak Minah switched the baby to her other arm and yelled at me, "Very good, fall down some more! Always careless! Never watch where you're going!"

'I bawled loudly. Hsian stood looking at me with a crimson face. Then, that strange Indian woman came and crouched in front of me and opened her arms wide. I walked into them, and she held me. She held me until I stopped crying. That moment, I just fell in love with her.'

'Fell in love?' Hsian's smile is grim. 'Girl, you literally moved in. If there'd been an extra bed, you'd have even slept in her house.'

'If she had, so what?' Auntie sniffs. 'She was always welcome. Just like you.' Auntie looks at me then. 'Hsian's mother paid me to look after him, true, but I loved him and you too. I never asked your mother for money, Farida.'

It's my face that's red now. My mother has never ever offered to pay Auntie Ruku anything in cash or kind, even though she knows Auntie Ruku needs money badly; even though I ate at her place, did my homework there, watched TV there, studied my lessons there and generally spent the entire day in her house. My Abah did suggest it, but Mak said: 'I'm not asking her to look after my child so why should I pay her? She wants to look after her, let her *lah*.'

'I love all of you,' Auntie says. 'I don't look at anybody as Chinese or Indian or Malay . . .'

Hsian places his hands on his head. His eyes go wide open. I know what he's thinking; I'm thinking the same thing too—adults are the pits in the way they practise self-deception. Racists are always other people and never themselves. He walks up to Auntie and kisses her on her head. 'Yeah, right. Wasn't it you who said that Puan Maimun is a typical lazy Malay teacher?'

I grin. Seizing the moment, I hug her from the back. 'And didn't someone we know say "That fella, typical Chinaman, nothing straight about him except his hair"?'

Auntie laughs and turns it into a cough. I suspect most people out there are like her; some of my teachers too. Arun once got into a huge fight with a new teacher when she called an Indian boy '*mabuk keling*'.

'Mabuk? Mabuk?' His voice dripped with scorn.

'Puan Latifah, it's 8.30 in the morning. How can he be drunk? How crazy is that?'

'Quiet!' Puan Latifah yelled.

Arun wouldn't be quiet. 'And why do you call us keling? You know it's a disgusting word, right? We're not keling, Puan Latifah. We're Malaysian.'

He was like that, carrying all insults like stab wounds on his body. Shitty remarks about Indians as gangsters. The blackness of Indian skin. Indian drunks. *Bodoh* Indians in the bottom classes. Keling was the worst; the one slur bandied about so frequently and by so many people, none of whom were ethnic Indians. Arun took them all personally, lashings on his body, day in and day out. Sometimes it made me tired.

The three of us would talk all the time about how adults were puffed up with their own grievances, their sense of victimhood. That was their tragedy. And we—we imitated them. That was ours. Anyways, no more already! Hsian, Arun, Farida. We were going to change the script. Out with race differentiation. In with equity, respect and acceptance. How on earth we were going to do that, we had no idea. Not yet.

There's a buzz from my phone in my pocket. It's a message from Zul:

IS HE ALL RIGHT? PLEASE TELL ME HE'S OKAY.

I'm touched. Zul has never clicked with either Arun or Hsian. I text back:

CAN'T SAY YET. STILL UNCONSCIOUS.

'You three. People say you're very good friends but *dey*, they don't see how you argue, always argue—Malaysian disease *lah*, this *lah*, that *lah*. And you never told me what that disease is. Diabetes, ah?'

Hsian smiles and shakes his head. He says, 'Auntie, you remember that time when we were talking about religion?'

'*Dey*, you're always arguing about religion. Made my head spin.'

I remember. I said mine was the best and the purest when Hsian made a little salute and said, 'All hail Buddhism!' That was rich, coming from an atheist.

Arun said, 'Hinduism has all the answers—that's why we have loads of crooked holy men!'

Auntie Ruku looked appalled. 'Crooked? I thought they were all saints!' And she grinned.

'They're evil Klingons!' Arun declared. Hsian jumped in with another salute. 'All hail the Klingons! Masters of the evil universe!'

'Evil Klingons!' Auntie remembers with a smile. She goes over to Arun and touches his head. 'It never mattered that you're not my son, not my nephew, not a relative at all—your mother was my friend. When your father died, she gave you to me to raise and went to Singapore to work as a security guard. More money in Singapore, you see, so she could support you better. Who thought she'd die in a robbery? Who thought?'

I do not breathe. 'I didn't know this, Arun, I swear. I thought she was your mother. You called her "*Amma*".'

I look at Hsian. He looks as shell-shocked as me.

'Always not enough money, however hard I tried to save my pension; but you know you filled all the empty spaces in my life, Arun, until these two children came along . . . and they made me so happy, made you happy. And if you die now, Arun, I will die too. That's all I want to say.'

She looks at me. 'You think this auntie's not very clever, but I tell you, your quarrel yesterday, it was not your anger doing the talking, it was your ego.' She shakes her head. 'You just wanted to demolish each other.'

That. Quarrel. We always thought we were immune to the Malaysian disease. We were the face of the brave new world, willing to fight prejudice and stare at the challenges straight in the eye. And we were going places. Arun thought he was too.

Auntie's face turns ashen. 'This boy, so clever and so foolish. Always thinking life's so easy, you can get anything just like that,' she snapped her fingers. 'Just like both of you. I told him, "Get real, boy. You cannot compare. She'll walk into a scholarship and Hsian's father will educate him, but you have to take whatever they give you in a government university—because I can't afford anything else."'

I squirm when she says that. I'm a brilliant Malay, yes, and I deserve the generous scholarship but still, there's always the lurking guilt, knowing why things are so much easier for me. Hsian's rich. His father plans to send him to Sydney to read economics. Arun applied for engineering, computer science and physics, in the government universities. He got consumer studies.

'I'll find something else,' he tossed his head. 'When you're the wrong colour, wrong religion, you got to think on your feet, or you'd be crushed into nothing. I'll be fine.' He didn't look fine. I should have zipped up, right? I opened my mouth.

'*Itulah*,' I said with a laugh. 'If only your name was Harun instead of Arun. You'd be waltzing into a scholarship just like me.'

'YOU THINK IT IS FUNNY?' he snarled at me.

'No, I didn't mean it that way, come on man . . .' I felt flustered.

'Chill, macha, chill,' Hsian stepped in.

'Don't tell me to chill, Hsian. You have no idea how I feel . . . This colour, this race, this face, this black skin . . .' He thumped his chest with his open palm. Slap. Slap. Slap. '. . . like being forever third class.'

'Sucks big time but we're going to change it, remember?' Hsian said.

'How, Hsian? They won't let us. You know how many interviews I've gone for? So, I can get a scholarship to a private university? Huh? Got enough rejections to bury me alive.' His voice rose. 'Look at my results—they couldn't even give me physics. Consumer studies. What the heck is that? Hussein got engineering—bloke can't even add properly, come on! Fatimah got veterinary science. Hah! Fatimah—the girl who runs a mile when she sees a dog.' He turned to me, his voice bitter. 'Your kind—you don't even have to study—it just gets handed to you on a plate.'

'My kind? *My kind?*' I couldn't believe my ears. Was this my best friend speaking? Did it all come down to this in the end? My kind. Versus yours. I felt a blinding fury surge through me.

What did I say? I remember fragments from both of us. 'You despise my kind? Go back to your own kind then. *Balik* India.'

'Balik India? Why should I? India is not my country. This is my country.'

We weren't screaming. We hissed loathing at each other.

'Pariah. Keling. Miserable black Indian. Always whining.'

'Entitled natives. Greedy, grasping, always wanting everything free of charge. Lazy. Shiftless.'

We stood facing each other, fangs bared. Unkind, contemptuous words. Where did they come from? I never ever dreamed we had caught them from the adults and kept them safe, nurtured in our bosoms.

Hsian tried to stop us. 'You're playing the same old rhetoric, both of you!' he cried. 'Change the game, you idiots. What's the matter with you?'

The matter was that the serpent had escaped from where it was—buried deep in our hearts—and had emerged, hungry and angry. Auntie rushed out of her room. She told us to shut up and reached out to touch my arm. That was when I swatted her hand off and stormed away.

No one was home except Zul who looked at my face that felt all mottled and hot. He was alarmed: 'Are you crying? Did something happen? What did Arun do?'

I wasn't crying right up until that point but when he mentioned Arun, all the hurt and betrayal spilled over. 'I don't want to hear his name!' I went into my room and shut the door, ignoring Zul who banged on it, yelling: 'Did he hurt you? Did he hurt you? Farida?'

'Go away!'

* * *

Auntie has gone to the washroom. I've been waiting for her to go because something's been niggling at the back of my mind, and I don't want her to hear it. 'Hsian, what happened really? All I know is you two were attacked at the basketball court in the playground last night.'

'No, I wasn't attacked, only him. I've told the police already.' His voice is flat, and he keeps his eyes on Arun. 'We were messing around, shooting hoops. No one else was there. We weren't really in the mood—after the quarrel and all that. After you left, we were sitting around, crushed. Auntie was crying. Arun picked up the phone several times to call you. He was bitterly ashamed. He didn't know what to tell you, but he called. You didn't answer.

'So, I was still messing around in the basketball court. Arun walked away and sat on the bench near the gate. I was bouncing the ball when it flew off into the hedge. I went looking for it. Then I heard yelling and scuffling. I turned back and saw a boy beating Arun with a helmet. He must have hit him from the back at first because Arun was on the ground, face down. He got up, unsteady, bleeding and he grappled with the boy. They rolled on the ground and the boy was howling and punching Arun. What chance did Arun have? That coward hit him on his head! Coward!' Hsian spits the word out. Hsian, shouting, ran towards them and the boy with one last kick at Arun, jumped on his motorbike and escaped.

I close my eyes. 'Did you recognize the boy?'

Hsian is silent. Then he says, 'Like I told the police, I was too far away.'

Something is not right. 'Why would he attack Arun? He didn't steal his wallet or his bag. What are you not telling me?' I grab his shirt. 'Was it someone you know?'

'I've told you what I told the police and Auntie Ruku. It was a random attack. And when he wakes up, that's exactly what Arun will say too.'

A strange dread rises in me, rising from my stomach to clutch my throat. I can't breathe. I can't see. I want to throw up. 'Hsian?' I whisper.

'I won't say anything more, Farida. Arun won't either.' I hear the raggedness in his words. 'It stops with us, you see. It has to bloody well stop with us.'

Auntie comes back. Hsian and I are sitting next to Arun's bed. I'm curled up in my chair, one hand on my knees, the other, wrapped in Hsian's hand. Hsian's other arm rests on my shoulder. Auntie tut tuts and says the stress has gotten to me. So she sits by my side too.

The Taste of Pickles

Cherrie Sing

Most of my classmates look forward to summer when the school year ends. Not me though. My summers are spent in our little auto-supply store in Binondo. My parents, especially my father, believe that letting children work in the store every summer helps them develop character. It is a necessary obligation of every child in the family, even if said fourteen-year-old baulks and would rather play basketball with his friends.

Did I mention there's no pay? And that I'm not allowed to bring my cell phone?

This summer is no different. I'm stuck again in our auto shop, sitting at the counter, staring at the dusty street outside. I hope none of my friends ever get to see me or smell the sweat off my armpits.

'Derik!'

Papa again. I turn around to see him fuming over my apparent uselessness. Sometimes I think, for some mysterious reason, he hates me. He gestures me over to his desk and slaps a folder on my hands.

'How are you ever going to learn if you just keep standing behind the counter? Here are some of the things you need to learn, starting with this price list,' he points to the folder in my hands. 'You need to know our products.'

He pauses for dramatic effect, glaring at me while I stare back woodenly at him.

There's no winning against Papa though, so I give in and start leafing through the price list, tidily arranged in a red plastic folder. Just then, something shiny blinds my eyes. I look up from the folder to the street, my hand shielding my eyes.

It is the reflection of sunlight bouncing off a chrome bumper of a maroon Mercedes Benz, 1960 model. It moves slowly, stopping, then parking in the space in front of our store. A driver, in a white polo shirt, alights and opens the rear passenger door for a woman and a girl.

The driver enters the store and clears his throat. 'The left rear wheel is a little soft. Do you have something for it? An air pump maybe? We're too far away from any gas station around here and we can't find any vulcanizing stores.'

Our man, Jose, surveys the wheel that the driver points out. 'It's not that soft.' He soon brings out a portable air-pump can. 'Just for emergencies. It's good for cases like this, as long as the air needed is not too much.'

The driver looks at the yellow can and passes it to the woman. She critically examines it and the attached red tube. She squints as she reads the label, tightly pursing her red mouth. She has a long, whitened face that is saturated with make-up powder, and her hair is pulled tightly in a bun that stretches her face. The way she reads the labels on the canister with her hands curved around it like talons, her long red fingernails clicking on the can, annoys me.

After what seems like a long time, she unhooks her fingers and pushes the bright yellow can towards the driver. She gives him an unblinking, stare that seems to convey her wishes and places her black bag on the counter.

'How much?' the driver askes.

'Three hundred and thirty,' Papa says briskly. As the woman takes out a 500-peso bill, Papa motions to me to write out a receipt, which I quickly do. Papa hands the change from the cash register to the woman.

The girl has clambered on to the stool at the other side of the counter and is trying to play with the canister. Her pigtails bob as she peers into the red tube attached to the nozzle. She is wearing a pink ballet dress with a high fluffy skirt.

'Stop that, Chloe. Just sit,' the woman slaps the girl's hands away and quickly passes the canister to the driver. Her lips are pursed so tightly they seem to be sinking into her mouth.

'I was just looking at it,' the girl pouts, her chin jutting out towards the woman.

They are speaking in English! Yet the woman answered Papa in Filipino when he asked them to wait inside the store while the men fixed the flat.

Outside, the driver is busy fixing the tire, with Jose teaching him how to use the canister. A big, dark man, dressed in a *barong*, hunkers alongside them while holding a walkie-talkie.

'Is this Chinatown?' the woman asks suddenly, speaking to me in English. She glares at me with her unblinking, squinty-black eyes.

I nod, and she continues, 'The heart of Chinatown?' she asks in English.

I shake my head and reply in English. 'The heart of Chinatown is Ongpin, a few blocks from here.' I gesture in the direction of the famous street.

'Oh,' she says, then looks around, taking in our cluttered store, then the dusty street it faces, with its clogged and dirty road gutters and smelly piles of garbage. Her tight lips curve into a sneer. 'Ongpin must really be dirty.'

It hurts to hear this stranger criticize the heart of the town where I live. And it hurts all the more because she has actually spoken the truth. Ongpin is a filthy, stinking street, its canals clogged with garbage, the sidewalks full of vendors and heavily polluted water passing beneath its bridges.

The woman brushes invisible dirt off her shoulder and I notice that she is wearing a bright blue shirt, silky and expensive. She gives Papa and me a cursory nod. 'We'll just wait in the car. Come on, Chloe.'

'But I don't want to,' Chloe whines. 'I want to ride a horse. Aren't there any horse carriages in Ongpin? Can we ride one today, Mom?' Chloe pleads.

'Not now.' The woman pulls her daughter to the car. 'This place is not safe.'

Chloe pulls back. 'I want to, Mom.' She stamps her foot then screams louder. 'I want to ride now!'

'Tell you what,' the woman's eyes dart left to right, trying to come up with an answer, 'we'll go to Tagaytay tomorrow so you can ride a real horse, okay?'

Chloe's eyes light up, and I marvel at how quickly the woman can promise something that big to her child. It is enough to satisfy the little girl that she lets her mom lead her to the car. I wonder—hadn't they planned anything for tomorrow?

Luckily, the car has been fixed and as they drive away from us, Jose looks at Papa. 'One of the guys is a bodyguard.'

'And they are English-speaking too, Papa.'

Papa merely shrugs and looks at the street. Finally, he says, 'That Benz of theirs is quite rare nowadays. It can fetch a lot of money.'

* * *

A few days later, some of my friends drop by unexpectedly to visit me. One of them is juggling a basketball playfully. They're all on their way to the house of one of my other friends to play.

'Derik, you sure look funny. I didn't know you wear commercial T-shirts in your store,' hoots one of my friends.

The others join in and laugh even harder when they notice I am wearing rubber flip-flops. As they walk away after chatting with me, I yearn to join them and play basketball. Instead, I try to keep my smile firmly in place as they wave goodbye to me.

'Well, it seems that all of your friends are a lot taller than you are,' Papa comments.

I turn away, pretending to read the price list.

In the corner of my eye, I see Papa staring at me and I try to ignore him. But then, his stare does not last long as his head suddenly whips in the direction of the street. Beside me, Jose hisses.

I look up and see another Mercedes Benz exactly the same as the one we saw last week. And from Papa's and Jose's looks, I realize it is the same car.

'PKL,' Jose says, reading the plate number.

The Benz double-parks in front of our store. The driver alights quickly and clears his throat noisily as he enters the store.

It's the same driver.

'Ma'am wants another of those pumps to keep in reserve,' he hands over the money.

Peering into the tinted shades of the Benz from my place at the counter, I see an outline of a sharp nose of the passenger sitting in the backseat and as far as I can tell, it seems to be a different person with short hair who is reading a book.

'Thank you.' The driver takes the change and receipt from Papa and hurries back to the Benz.

Papa heaves a sigh of relief after they leave.

* * *

There are two people who come to the store regularly. Meme, my sister, comes every Wednesday afternoon after her math class. Her name isn't actually Meme; her real name is Elizabeth. But I call her Meme simply because she's my younger sister.

Meme is here earlier than usual today and making a nuisance of herself. Right now, she's sitting on my chair at the counter, eating a club sandwich and dropping a lot of crumbs.

'Meme, don't sit on my chair! Don't you have something to do?' I try to be obvious in shooing her away from my seat.

'It's not my fault the teacher didn't come today and that there was no substitute teacher around,' she says to me, her chin jutting out pugnaciously, daring me to question her.

For a brief moment, I remember the girl with the woman and the Benz.

'Advance summer classes are no fun,' Meme says, pouting. 'Why didn't Papa and Mama let you take advance classes?'

'Because you're the smart one, and you like to study. Besides, I'm needed at the store.'

Actually, that's not true. Meme has difficulty in math and having advance math classes for the next grade level can help her. And I'm in the store because Papa just likes making me miserable during summers.

Meme looks around. The men were packing stocks in boxes for deliveries. Then, she looks at me.

'I don't see you doing anything.'

'That's because you're in my seat. I'm supposed to be reading the price list.'

I don't think Meme believes me, because her eyes are on her sandwich. Her face crinkles in disgust and I know she's going to ask me a favour. She starts batting her eyes, smiling hopefully.

'Could you please eat the pickle for me?' Meme is now really into her beautiful-eyes routine.

'No. You should learn to eat them.'

Nevertheless, she removes the pickle from her sandwich and hands it to me. I hate pickles, but I've learned to eat them even though I don't like them. When I reached the age of ten, Papa refused to eat the pickles from my sandwiches and told me to learn to eat them. And so I did, because it is wasteful to throw it away.

I try to catch Papa's attention, but he is on the phone with a client. Reluctantly, I take the pickle and quickly pop it into my mouth. 'Thank you,' Meme says solemnly, nodding, as if I had just eaten the communion host. She is trying to be cute. I frown, remembering the little girl named Chloe, looking cute and very spoiled.

'It's the last time I eat your pickles,' I say, as the sourness floods into my mouth. 'I don't like them either.'

* * *

Mr Lim, Papa's friend, visits almost every Friday to chat with Papa. He's older than Papa by a few years and gives Papa advice, whether solicited or not. He's also an amusing raconteur. Whenever he gets excited about the topic on hand, his voice takes on a lilt and his hands perform all sorts of exaggerated motions.

'I counted five banks!' Mr Lim raises an arm and I'm reminded of the way our principal delivers speeches during our general assembly. 'Five banks on this small block of yours!' he continues to yell. 'And I haven't counted the ones on the other half of the street and the intersecting one.'

'There's more,' Papa adds. 'Do you see the construction going on in the corner over there?' Papa points. 'That's going to be a bank.'

'*Wah-pay-lo!* Another bank? Why, I also passed by construction two blocks from here and there was a sign on it saying that was going to be a bank.' Mr Lim is just warming up; he is rubbing his hands. 'It's an exaggeration—the way people think that all Chinese here in this district are rich,' Mr Lim shakes his head.

'If only they knew,' Papa laments. 'Ordinary businessmen like us cannot afford the rents any more. They keep on increasing. The banks can afford to pay though, and that's why there are so many of them here. Look at me,' Papa points to himself. 'I pay the rent for this store and I still worry about other expenses. Land prices in this area are too much; I can't afford to buy.'

'How much do you pay anyway?'

Papa doesn't reply.

Mr Lim whistles. 'I can guess.' He pauses, tilting his head on one side as he moistens his lips. 'You ever see the ad with the slogan "Patronize Filipino stores"? With the word "Filipino" underlined? I don't see why they have to do that. What are they implying?'

Papa rolls his eyes. 'Don't ask. Our Chinese neighbour from the mainland told me we aren't even real Chinese.'

'Then what does that make us?' Mr Lim spits. 'Maybe we should all go and buy an island and declare independence, like Singapore.'

I have to laugh at that. Mr Lim turns to laugh with me. 'Hey, your son is big. *Yen taw ah.*'

Papa's mouth stretches into a thin line. '*Aya*! He's too skinny. And useless.'

'*Tung-twa ba*! Kids go through stages like this,' Mr Lim nods at me.

Meanwhile, Papa picks up a ringing phone, frowning, his disappointment in me showing.

* * *

Monday afternoon. Our street in front of the store has few cars parked at the kerb. The heat of the afternoon sun, coupled with the inactivity of doing nothing, has made me bored. I prop my elbows on the counter to stare outside the shop.

Something glitters in my peripheral vision. It's the old maroon Mercedes Benz again, cruising down our quiet street. My skin begins to prickle as it slows down at the store.

The driver gets out and hands us the can he bought from us a week ago. It's dented, light and obviously empty.

'We would like to return this. When we tried to use it, nothing came out. No air.'

Papa shakes his head. 'When we gave that to you it was intact. You saw and received the item with your own hands. This can looks obviously used.'

'A refund,' the driver insists. 'Here's the receipt.'

Papa gasps. The receipt indicates that the price of the can is 880 pesos. 'You only paid 330 pesos for this can. You overpriced it?'

'I did not.' The driver bites his lip.

As Papa and I browse through the duplicate receipts, the woman comes out of the car. She is wearing a blouse that looks like it has real diamonds on it. In a high-pitched voice, she asks, 'Are you going to refund or not?'

'No,' Papa's eyes are steely. 'We sold the item in good condition in the first place.' Papa brings out the duplicate copy for the woman to see. 'Secondly, we sold it for 330 pesos only. Your driver overpriced it.'

'My husband is a congressman,' the woman says, straightening her posture. 'If you do not pay me the full amount of 880 pesos, I will make sure that your business will be destroyed. Your name will be tarnished and you will go to jail.' She slaps an ID on the counter, showing the details of a congressional office in the city of a Metro Manila district. 'You're not a real Filipino anyway. It will be easy to deal with you.' Her face looks disdainful as her eyes sweep over our store name and frontage.

Papa stands looking uneasy, his eyes darting from the domineering figure of the woman to the ID before him. When the woman's burly bodyguard sidles up close behind her, he shows off the gun hanging at his belt.

Papa opens his mouth, about to say something. Go, Papa, go, I beg silently. She doesn't have the right to do this to us. We are in the right here. Fight for our rights too, Papa; even if we may look like foreigners, we still live here, we—

My thoughts go no further as Papa tells me, 'Get the amount from the cash register.'

I look at him, stunned. This isn't what I expect Papa to say. I want him to do something more, to fight back or even just stand up for our rights. Isn't that what the school has taught us on what we, as citizens, can do?

'Now, Derik!' Papa orders sharply.

Numbly, I obey, taking out the exact amount of money from the cash drawer with deliberate slowness.

'Faster,' the woman shouts. Inwardly I curse her and all the people like her, who use their political power only to coerce and abuse others. As I hand the money to her, she snaps it quickly from my fingers like a hungry dog.

'You're fired,' she tells the driver. 'I'm going to file your name in the NBI and make sure you never get a job again.'

The driver cowers in fear as the bodyguard assists her to the car. Assuming the driver's seat, the bodyguard drives away with her.

We stare at the Benz as it drives away. The driver has slunk away from our store. Papa is breathing heavily while I stand beside him, the taste of dry, sour pickles on my tongue.

Broken Filaments

Paul GnanaSelvam

1986 finally comes to a wrap. Today, the primary section of my school is celebrating the postponed Children's Day event, which is also the last day of the school calendar before the long, year-end holiday begins. There is chaos all around me in the changing room, as teachers are busy prepping us for the talent show that is going to start in an hour to mark the celebrations.

'I've been selected for a sketch, *Amma*,' I told my mother this morning when she asked me why I needed her saree.

'What do boys have to do with a saree?' she asked suspiciously.

'We are dressing up as butterflies, Ma. The story is about a group of insects trying to survive winter,' I answered thoughtfully.

'And you are a butterfly?' she mocked laughingly as she handed me a dark blue silk saree, bordered with curvy mangoes woven in gold thread. I took it with a heavy heart and packed it in a paper bag. It was one of her favourites, I knew. Only mothers gave their best and without reservations.

'Make sure it doesn't get tainted, or the thread pulled out,' she cautioned as I left home.

News seems to have gotten around the school that the talent show included boys being dressed up as women. A large crowd has gathered to see the transformation taking place in the dressing room. Peering through the window shutters, a large group of boys have started making the ubiquitous remarks that I am so accustomed to.

'Eh *pondan*,' shouts one boy to which another resonates with a distinct '*potteh*'. Shaking their heads, the teachers exchange glances with sheepish giggles.

Our class teacher, Miss Begum, has somewhat tastefully selected me, Jeyapragash, Danny Lim and Suhairy, for the beauty pageant. Suhairy is smiling shyly as *Cikgu* Ainon tries to fasten the *kerongsang* along the buttons of his *baju kebaya*. He seems to be enjoying all the attention he is getting. He has even brought a complete set of matching accessories for his dress, including a gold necklace, a brooch and beaded slippers with low heels.

'Stay still,' Cikgu Ainon admonishes Suhairy, doing her best to fit the skinny boy into a woman's dress.

Danny Lim is standing almost numb in a tight-fitting cheongsam while getting a shiny, black wig to cover his crew cut. He is definitely grumpy about the heat and his new-found suit is threatening to burst at the seams. Dressed in a black gown, Jeyapragash, on the other hand, is chatting incessantly with Miss Lai, who is drawing on his eyelids with an eyeliner.

'You have very nice hips,' compliments Miss Begum as she drapes the six yards of silk around my waist.

I do not know what to make out of it or how to respond to her. I am big-boned and usually join the tall and big-sized guys who typically occupied the last-row desks in the classroom. However, I am rounder than the other boys. At eleven, I have a big belly and bigger buttocks. These features are complemented with extra mounds of flesh that have grown around my chest, something that is absent among the other boys. When they developed, my parents freaked out, fearing to be cancer. On top of that, my soft demeanour and flabby thighs, which pulled my legs together when I walked, did not help. I became conspicuous in school.

'Large enough to hold the pleats,' Cikgu Ainon agrees with her.

'The fabric drapes perfectly over his behind,' chirps Miss Begum. Then, she takes hold of the artfully folded pleats and instructs me to take a deep breath. She pulls the buckle away from my belly button and tucks the pleats between my navel and my shorts.

'There,' she says and makes long pleats of the *munthani* with the free end of the cloth before pinning it on to the school shirt's sleeve over my left shoulder. 'Why are you sweating?' she asks and pulling out a tissue from her handbag, proceeds to wipe my eyelids and lips. 'Ah, blue will look good on you,' she decides, as she extracts a small brush from her bag and dabs sparkling blue powder on my eyelids. Then it's time for the rouge, tarnishing my dark skin with a pink glow. I fidget when she twirls open her maroon lipstick, but she grasps my chin firmly between her thumb and finger.

Looks like I have successfully amassed a group of rowdy fans. I notice a group of Indian boys gathered on the other side of the room. '*Dei, ombothu,*' one of them screeches, and the others laugh. I know him. He's Kugan from the next class.

Somehow, they've learnt to equate nine to being incomplete unlike ten, signifying the hormonal imbalance in me.

'Have you no other work?' Kugan asks. 'You just wait, I'll catch you after school and give you a good punch,' he warns.

Danny Lim looks at me and shakes his head. 'Have some decency,' he yells at Kugan. But it falls on deaf ears. 'Their England sure no good one!' he says to console me.

'I am supposed to be a butterfly!' I want to shout back but realize it won't do any good. I'm here because I couldn't say no to Miss Begum. Finally, two fake earrings are clipped to my earlobes and I am actually thanking my lucky stars that Miss Begum has forgotten to bring the stick-on *pottus*. She asks me to take a seat with the rest of the boys who are already dressed as Gandhi, Napoleon Bonaparte, Julius Caesar, Tunku, Sudirman and various uniformed personnel such as soldiers, doctors, policemen, firemen and construction workers. They are cocky and avoid eye contact with Jeyapragash, Danny Lim, Suhairy and me. Conceding rejection, I join my friends who are supposed to portray social harmony in the likes of Rani, Leeza, Ah Mei and Soraya, and render a patriotic song. The vertical pleats of the saree keep getting trapped under my canvas shoes and make me stumble. So, I lift the pleats up and walk over to the waiting area. That is when I hear Miss Begum calling out '*gundu mamee*' to a cackle of laughter from the teachers behind me. I walk on, without turning back or smiling.

'Fat aunty,' announces Jeyapragash as I sit down beside him.

'D'you think he doesn't know that?' Danny Lim stares him down.

The other Indian boys continue with their antics. Encouraged by the others, Devendran, my classmate, is making noises that resemble a cat in heat. Purring, he asks if

I want to join him. At one point, Kugan pelts me with a small stone. When I turn to look at him, Devendran and Kugan are acting out an obscene scene, touching each other, mimicking kissing and humping against each other like street dogs. The small crowd goes mad with raucous laughter, enjoying the ribaldry. I draw the ends of the saree over my head in shame.

My cheeks are burning, and my stomach is churning. A makeshift stage has been erected in the car park outside the dressing room. The rain trees that line the compound provide the much-needed shade. Unfortunately, the end of the car park also leads to the gates of the primary school, where parents and school buses are waiting to fetch the students. The parents are already lining up along the fence, enjoying the performances. All this unwanted attention is making me so nervous that my legs and hands feel paralysed. The drying makeup, like multiple layers of crayon, is turning my skin into plastic crusts. I begin to dread that someone I know will see me in a saree, especially my cousin, Raj. This would make it worse as Raj has already gotten into this nasty habit of grabbing me from behind and squeezing my breasts until I gasp for air. It was also Raj who had complained to Amma that I was befriending effeminate boys in school. This embarrassing news would definitely reach the ears of my grandmother and aunty. Amma would find out that I did not flutter on stage like a butterfly, after all. In fact, she would find out that her son had metamorphosed into one! There is a real danger that Amma could die of grief after that.

But Raj is nowhere to be seen as he is in the secondary school now. His school session starts in the afternoon. I take a deep breath. After the headmaster's speech, the talent show begins. The first performance is a combat scene, one that we are all too familiar with—fighting the communists, Japanese and then Independence. The stage must be really warm because the Tunku and the soldiers in green baggy suits return to the dressing room drenched in perspiration.

We find out that we are last in the line-up for the day. 'The best for the last,' announced Mr Ho, the emcee for the event. He pats our shoulders, his swerving palms moving almost like a falling leaf.

'I don't know why I agreed to this,' sighs Jeyapragash, suddenly nervous.

'It's her idea,' retorts Danny Lim, nudging his chin towards Miss Begum, who is now seated with the teachers in the front row.

'She's the class teacher, how to say no?' Suhairy asks, adjusting the long sleeves of his kebaya on his skinny elbows. 'She would have slapped us if we did not agree.'

Standing at four-and-a-half feet, with curly hair, Miss Begum looks like a stiff doll. Her powdered face is separated from her neck by different complexions. The boys always wondered whether she owned 365 Punjabi suits, where she lived and why she owned a German Shepherd despite her religion. She is infamous for her strict ways, often dubbed the lioness of Zambezi in our fifth standard. With a phlegmy, but loud voice, and a thick cane that she wields like a magic wand, she commands attention, bringing the biggest and the most notorious boys to their knees. When she does not carry a cane, her strong fists and unusually flat palms do the trick, dubbed as the '3Ps'—palming (slapping), pinching (the soft love handles) and pulling (the sideburns, before, palming). I hate her because I am not good at algebra and more so because I was tasked to buy her lunch during recess time.

'What's wrong with you?' Danny Lim implores annoyingly, cooling himself vigorously with a paper fan.

'At least we get to do this, once outside of our rooms.' He produces a hysterical laugh. Suhairy and Jeyapragash laugh along with their mouths covered and nod.

I am not laughing with them. I am trembling at the large spectre of apprehension looming over me. The dressing room is now empty except for the four of us, as the other boys have left after their own segments ended. I feel a wave of embarrassment engulfing me. This saree that I am draped in is not working for me.

I keep asking myself, why I am doing this? Why should I be called names, ridiculed by others and mocked? This scene will be committed to everyone's memories even next year, after I come back to Standard Six. This memory of me in a saree will not be erased from the minds of those who call me names and their taunts will carry on for years to come. And then, the shuddering thought arrives: what if . . . what if . . . Raj is among the audience? The loud rowdy applauses might have reached all parts of the school. Raj might have heard about the four of us. And he might have clambered out from his waiting spot before his session started and come over to catch some entertainment.

I decide I am not taking part in this—not at my expense. I gather up the pleats and hold them tightly. Danny Lim turns to me, his expression changed.

'What? Now? You must be kidding,' he says.

'Toilet?' Suhairy asks, concerned. Jeyapragash gives me a sympathetic look.

'Just go,' says Danny Lim, waving me away.

I hold the jumble of folded fabric protruding from my belly and walk out before anyone stops me—especially Mr Ho. The toilet is gloomy and reeks of urine, but it is a welcome relief as there is no one in sight. It is my sanctuary for now. I am not taking part in any pageantry. I have suffered enough. Not even Miss Begum is going to make me appear in a saree, like a woman. I will never give the school tyrants a reason to torment me. I will never let my friends down. I will never let my mother down.

I walk straight into the last cubicle, past the urinals, and fasten the latch. Mosquitoes take flight and give me room to lean against the scribbled walls. My heart is beating frantically, and finally, I release the pleats to the floor. When I look down, I see the blue and gold saree is sweeping over a patch of stools. I panic. Without thinking, I quickly unravel the pleats of the soft textile, dropping them on to the toilet floor altogether. Then I realize that I cannot retrieve it, regardless of the consequences it could bring. Disgusted, I push the now soggy pile of cloth further into the crevasse of the toilet pan, pull the flush and get out of the cubicle in time for the gurgling water to consume it. At once, I feel lighter. The pungent smell and the sight of the long gritty washroom do not bother me. The emptiness is a welcome relief. I stand in front of the uneven mirrors to take a look at my painted face as the announcements penetrate into the toilet, loud and clear, through its air wells. It is Mr Ho.

'And now,' he begins ceremoniously, 'I would like to welcome our own Charlie's Angels.'

The crowd is cheering so loudly that the glass shutters of the air well chime along. 'Wait a minute,' he pauses to count. 'There is one more, where is the *thanggachi*?' He questions playfully. 'We are supposed to have four. I saw him just now,' he is looking for someone. But the crowd is impatient. So, they continue cheering for the three performers walking out on to the stage. While I wonder whether I should lock myself again in the cubicles, Mr Ho announces that there is no time to look for the fourth sister. He invites Danny Lim, Jeyapragash and Suhairy to start singing. Soon, '*Burung Kakak Tua*'—a song taught during music lessons about an old parrot singing without its teeth—is sung amidst the loud applause of the excited audience. Whatever happened to the manly and stoically sung national anthem? Did my friends or someone change their minds?

I remove the earrings and toss them into the dustbin. Now, I must remove the colour coated on to my face—attached like a stubborn mask—before I can even think of going home. I wash, but it isn't easy to get rid of it. I scrub as hard as I can with my nails, but the dissolving paint only smudges my face further. After a few attempts, it remains on my dark smooth skin as a purplish patch. I must have been at it for a while, so focused that I did not realize that the singing had stopped and that all three of my friends are standing right behind me.

'Quick, before the monsters find us here,' shouts Danny Lim and disappears into a cubicle. Suhairy and Jeyapragash rip away their costumes and stash them into their plastic bags. Then all three start washing away their own makeup along with me at the sink.

'You escaped, didn't you?' Jeyapragash accuses me, his eye shadow forming a large red ring around his eyes. 'You deserted us,' he sneers.

'Very clever,' applauds Danny Lim, pointing to my shirt. I look down in dismay to see pink, blue and maroon splotches all over my starched, white shirt. 'Good luck,' he says.

Suhairy hugs me, 'the lioness,' he whispers into my ears. 'She was fuming, not very pleased. She was asking for you.'

Danny Lim shrugs his shoulders. As an afterthought, he says, 'good thing you weren't there.' Sighing deeply, he continues, 'let's go back to class, the day's not over yet.'

'Where is your saree?' asks Suhairy.

I point towards the cubicles.

Boys are on a rampage all over the school compound, smearing gold dust and flour on one another. As I reach the classroom, loud murmurs arise and Miss Begum looks up. Miss Begum, who does not tolerate absentees and unfinished homework and reduces the toughest boys to tears, gives me a kind smile and turns away without any questions.

'That's funny,' Danny Lim warns me.

Choruses of 'Auld Lang Syne' begin to fill up the hot afternoon air. Because Miss Begum did not approve of rowdyism, we are detained in the classroom. Suddenly, she announces that she has an idea. She picks a few boys and calls them to the front and asks them questions. The first two are the class monitor and assistant class monitor. When she has no mood to ask the usual questions about their hobbies, their pets, their favourite food, their ambitions, et cetera, she opens it to the class. Knowing how boys are, more interesting questions pop up about girlfriends and other titillating queries that are accompanied by roars of laughter and excitement. Just when I am about to duck my head, she calls for me.

'We've not seen much of you lately,' she says.

If I am not mistaken, Miss Begum is sitting up straight and looking gleeful, munching on peanuts from a bowl on her table. The class is already excited, with hands going up before I even walk up and turn myself in.

Shamsul Nizam throws the first stone. 'Why does everyone call you pondan?' he asks innocently.

I am dumbfounded. The boys are getting more adamant now. More hands are shooting up. I turn around for salvation, hoping Miss Begum would say something to spare my dignity. I am sure by now she knows where all these remarks are leading. Our eyes meet, but she looks away. Peanut crumbs escape her carved mouth. I think she is going to belch soon.

'Next question,' she says instead, turning to smile at me. My legs are wobbly and all I want is to hide somewhere, but Miss Begum will have none of that. I stand, trying to smile, looking for an answer. Amarjeet Singh, the non-turbaned, asthmatic Punjabi boy with bad breath speaks up from the desk in front of the class.

'Why d'you walk like a girl?' he asks in a singsong tone. I cannot take this. A deafening roar freezes me. Some of the boys are drumming on their desks. I feel defeated. But I am not taking this any more; the shame in me is turning into rage. When I turn again for solace from Miss Begum, I find that she is almost toppling off her chair with laughter.

'"Why d'you walk like a girl?" he asked,' she repeats to my deep sorrow. 'Gundu mamee,' she teases cruelly.

My universe shatters at this point. I disintegrate, feeling like I had been cut into pieces by unseen knives. My heart aches, my breaths are heavy and cold sweat is pouring out from every pore, making me dizzy. Tears well up in my eyes. I get dangerous. Almost in a trance, I lunge at Amarjeet Singh, landing my heavy fist right on his nape. My knuckles crack and I think I have fractured my wrist. Nevertheless, I raise my hand to strike him again. He scurries for cover behind Miss Begum, with tears dropping in grey splotches on his school uniform. The entire class cowers in dead silence. I stand in front of all the boys and burst out sobbing. Nobody comes to my aid, especially the Indian boys who teased me—not even Danny Lim, Jeyapragash or Suhairy.

Miss Begum stops laughing. She gets up from her chair hurriedly and says something, her mouth moving in circular motions like a washing machine, but it's mostly inaudible now. She is pointing to Amarjeet Singh who is staring at me like a wounded hawk. I disdainfully ignore them, sit down at my desk and bury my face in my hands. I am fairly sure Kugan won't wait for me outside the school compound now.

Time is the only comrade who stayed by me during the most exposed moment in my life. It gave me the space to gather myself. I do not remember the school bell ringing, but the class is now empty. I gather up my school bag and water container, mindful of the soiled saree I am leaving behind in the school toilet. I will think of an excuse on my way home. What would I do with the blue silk saree with the golden embroidery, anyway?

Diwali Lights

Adwiti Subba Haffner

Ramesh squatted on the floor and from under the bed against the window, which overlooked the dirt road that led to the main street of the neighbourhood, he pulled out the kerosene stove.

Ramesh went to work earlier than most people. Before he went to work every morning and while he cooked his meal every evening, he saw shoes going up and down the dirt road from his window. An old, brown, burlap curtain, which he drew only in the night, hung over the window. During the day, the window was the only source of light, barring the main and only door which he kept shut for the sake of privacy.

From his vantage point, he had the unique privilege of recognizing every shoe and its owner in the neighbourhood that walked past his window. Ramesh had been living in this little town, away from his '*desh*' for more than forty-three years now.

'It's colder than our desh,' the softly whispered words left her shy lips. These were the first words she had ever said to him when they alighted from the toy train, her eyes downcast, the end of her sari covering most of her face.

'Yes, but you'll get used to it. The people here, although we may not step inside their homes or mingle with them freely, are polite and soft-spoken. We're not allowed into temples, so just make sure you pray from outside; but besides that, we live inside the neighbourhood, not on the outskirts as we did in our hometown.' He had wanted to see her whole face without the veil, but she had been withdrawn until she became pregnant.

He carefully detached the circular outer cover of the stove, wiped away the soot on it with his sleeves. With eyebrow tweezers, which stayed hooked to the handle on the side of the stove, he gently pulled the wicks further up, so he could light them all. He was used to the smell of kerosene. In fact, he welcomed it after continuously smelling other people's garbage and outhouses all day long.

After lighting the wicks, he replaced the circular cover and the wicks lit up. It warmed up his 200-square-foot room and home quite instantly, like an expected hug from someone dear. He rummaged underneath the left side of his bed. From an old tin box, he measured a handful of rice; then dug his hand into a plastic jar and grabbed a fistful of yellow lentils which he placed inside a deep dish. It made a sound like ball bearings dropped on to a metal surface.

'Gopal passed his matriculation. With the cash I have saved under the mattress, we can send him to college. Maybe we need to ask how to go about it, particularly someone who lives in our neighbourhood; the kind *Babu* with glasses perhaps?'

'You mean Police Babu? Oh, I went to him today and the most unbelievable thing happened.'

Her eyes met his, the end of her sari, not used as a veil now but wound around her neck, like a scarf.

'What?' she asked, flipping over the puffed-up chapattis on the stove and then deftly tossing it up into the air so it dropped into a steel bowl.

'He was having breakfast and he asked me to sit with him at the dining table.'

'What? Really? Really?' Her eyes opened wide, a broad smile on her face. 'God bless him and his children.' She turned towards Police Babu's house with eyes closed and hands folded in prayer.

'Yes, when Police Babu was living in the police quarters, the time his house was being renovated, Lal Singh, my friend, took his four kids to school in the morning and collected them after school. Desh was different; we weren't even allowed to make eye contact with the higher castes. I am happy for Gopal; I want him to study and get his graduation and get a government job here.'

His eyes smarted with the memory of his wife, and how she had breathed her last before his very eyes at Eden hospital. 'Anaemia,' the doctor had said. He remembered how her hands and feet were always so cold, but he had attributed that to the mountain weather. His heart ached just as when he was first struck by her beauty at their wedding, only this time it was the excruciating pain of missing her presence. He added water, turmeric and some salt into the simmering mixture. He lifted the skirt of the bed cover, exposing more under his bed. In a small wicker basket, he found a red onion and an old potato. He smiled. He was in luck; his meal was going to taste better than yesterday. He peeled both, chopped them directly over the top of the pot, using his thumb as a cutting board, and dropped them into the boiling pot of rice and lentils. His little room was filled with the smell of his *khichdi*. His mouth started to water. It had been a long day.

Ramesh was seventeen when he arrived from Bihar to this mountain town, looking for a better life and friendlier people. 'Life is better in the hills; the caste system is not as severe as in our villages. Ramesh, you go make some money and send some home to us. There is hardly any work here. I cannot feed so many mouths and I still have to get your two sisters married. They're going to destroy me! I heard that there is a group of Harijans going to Siliguri, Dooars and Darjeeling. They had heard about some job openings for toilet cleaners in the railway department.'

He had to lift the latch of the right door to align the cleats perfectly before he could unlatch the door and fling it open to let the evening come snaking into his little room and settle into his kismet.

'Hey Ramesh, how is it going?' Mr Gurung asked him, resting his hip on his black umbrella.

'Oh Gurungji, namaskar . . . namaskar.' Ramesh's voice always took an obsequious tone when talking to anyone not his caste. It was an ingrained habit from his village. Caste was hammered into his DNA, like an animal branded with heated metal. With folded arms, Ramesh replied in pure Nepali but with a Bihari accent. 'Son Gopal and his family have left for desh to visit his in-laws for Diwali. I stayed back to keep earning money for the rent they have to pay for their apartment.'

'Are you celebrating Diwali with your people?' Mr Gurung asked solicitously.

'Oh Gurungji, there are not many families here. Most have gone back to desh for the pujas. One other family invited me, but you know we are poor people; I don't want them to have another mouth to feed, especially during the festival season.' He answered with hands still folded and with a slight smile on his face.

'I see. Good. Good. Make sure tomorrow you come to our house to collect our garbage. There will be lots of guests all day long.'

'Yes, sir, I will.' Ramesh folded his hands and watched Mr Gurung pace down to his green, freshly painted cottage down the slope. Ramesh adjusted his dhoti and breathed in the fresh autumn air that rapped at his aching bones.

An adept mist, alive in its movements, enveloped the emerging purple-hued evening, wrapping the vivacious sparkles that lit up waves and waves of tacit hills. After all these years of cleaning latrines and collecting garbage from houses, the smell lingered on not just on his clothes but on him, his very identity. In the forty-three years he had lived here in this neighbourhood, no one had ever set foot in his house. This was his life. This was what he had come to accept and expect.

The Bengali couple who lived above his room was having a heated discussion. There were rumours that the husband had tortured the wife by stubbing burning cigarette butts on the backs of her hands. Ramesh had heard this from the neighbourhood gossip while fetching water from the tap stand. He often saw her nervous, fast-paced feet moving briskly past his window. Her presence and gait seemed accidental, as if she had fallen into this area in an impetuous moment.

Through the thick invading mist, Ramesh heard the sound of a violin. The police officer with his four children lived just across the main artery of the neighbourhood and every evening, the sound of the violin mingled with the progression of the night.

From his room, each droplet of the mist clung on to the sweet, turmeric flavour of his khichdi and coerced him in.

Ramesh glanced at the small bottle of mustard oil by the windowsill and reached out to pour some but stopped short, looked at the bright, amber-coloured liquid and put it back. He had to light some *diyas* the next day.

Turning off the stove, he quickly moved it outside for the fumes were almost as unbearable as his loneliness. But, unlike the fumes, he could not simply carry his loneliness outside the door and expect the elements to absorb it all.

'I want to go for Diwali this year. I have saved some money under our mattress. I want to see my mother and father. I received a letter today from Tejpal that Father is not doing too well,' she had said, walking towards the mattress and had leafed through some worn-out one- and five-rupee notes.

'How do I look?' Ramesh reached for his mustard-coloured turban and wrapped it around his head.

She had smiled at him with a familiar warmth and excitedly dragged suitcases which served as drawers and closets from underneath the bed and pulled out carefully folded, bright *ghagras* and dhotis.

'When we go home, we have to dress up in our finest attire,' she had said, dusting the musky smell of mildew and moths.

Ramesh ate his meal quietly, directly from the pan, making scraping and scratching sounds as he neared the end of his dinner. He thought of his son and his newly wedded wife taking the train to Bihar. Then he washed the pan outside his door, a little to the left and gargled with the same water, spitting it out into the open drain that ran along the outer wall of his dwelling. Water was always scarce.

'Would you please buy me a bucket? Balancing water on my head was easier in the plains; here I have to climb up the steep, cliff-hugging trail to get water from the spring.' Eyes still looking down and voice yet timid and hesitant, she had requested him.

The All India Radio blared loudly 'I am a Disco Dancer'. After lowering the volume, he moved the knob to change stations, listening to short, ten-second samples, until he settled for some *bhajans*.

Ramesh fell asleep, praying that his son would get a promotion so he could retire and go back to his desh to die; but digging deeper he observed that he had been away for so long that he was estranged from his kith and kin there, he loved this little town, now his home, but there was a haunting emptiness inside his heart, a sense of restlessness that spun itself into a state of constant abeyance, a feeling that was subsumed into the density of nowhere now—not here, not there. A single teardrop left his left eye.

From his little cave, he was woken up by the tolling of the temple bells, devotees making their presence felt in the valley, announcing their arrival, summoning the goddess of wealth, Laxmi. It was the day goddess Laxmi was worshipped with great pomp and ceremony.

After performing his ablutions, Ramesh pulled out an incense stick from a blue-and-white box marked 'Nag Champa', burned it and making mini circles with the fragrant smoke he stabbed an orange with the tail-end of the incense stick, converting the fruit into an instant incense burner, and let the rest of the stick smoulder in one corner of his room.

With such stark furnishings, the fragrance meandered happily to the wooden table and chair in one corner of the room and that single shelf that was stacked with a few plates and some utensils. He picked up his broom and bucket, which was always placed next to the door, and left for work.

It was evening by the time he had completed his rounds and his work was done. He had collected Rs 10 that day as tips. He was going to buy a toy for his grandchild for Diwali.

Carrying some tiredness in his heart and some *pedas* that he had bought from the popular store Narayan Das in one hand and a different type of *sel rotis* that were gifted to him by various people he worked for on the other, he trudged home, letting the blooming of the diyas expunge his tiredness and blossom in his heart.

The cerulean twilight glowed with Diwali lights. Every house was decorated with hundreds of diyas, wrapping the doorways, patios and terraces. The whole town was sketched with a brush made of light. The distant hills looked like waves of fireflies fluttering in colonies, lights giving birth to more lights, illuminating every curve and camber of the city. Almost every main door was ajar ushering in the goddess, hoping this year would be the year they would be graced by the blessing of the elusive goddess Laxmi.

The cool air felt tender yet edgy, each movement of the breeze that he encountered brought with it the potency and spur of his own youth, the fervour of his life once when he would race home to be with his veiled bride, who spoke his language and had a soft, warm body. She had transported desh with her presence and supplied him with the familiar smells, sounds and feel of home.

Every year he heard *Bhailini*, the song sung by groups of girls who went from door to door every year during Diwali, blessing each household with their presence and their performance. Ramesh often wondered what it would be like to have these girls sing at his doorstep and sanctify his house too.

'*Bhailini ayew agana . . . baralee kuralii rakhana . . . aaah ausee ko deena gai tiwaro bhailo . . . bhailo . . . bhailo bhundai ayew, Laxmi puja pujdai ayew* . . . (Bhailini has come in your courtyard; clean your house and receive us . . . it is a new moon tonight; it is the festival of lights . . . today is the dark fortnight; let us worship Laxmi with delight).'

A group had gathered outside a house, two doors down from his lodging. It was a Tibetan magistrate's house; they too had lit diyas all along the edges of their veranda.

Ramesh was aware that people found his presence inauspicious, especially when the pujas were commencing, so he slunk away, hugging the opposite side of the path to be as inconspicuous as possible and quietly slipped into his one-room tenement.

Picking up the ashes from the devotional act in the morning, he burned three incense sticks this evening. He looked up at the shelf, and from behind the plates, he took out diyas. He carefully filled them with the oil he had not used the day before for his dinner and added six wicks made from cotton wool. He lit each one, muttering a prayer to Laxmi. He placed two diyas on the table and four in front of his house and pushed his door slightly ajar.

Removing from the wall a small picture frame of Goddess Laxmi, bedecked with gold and blessing gestures, he placed it on the table with the tea lights flanking her.

The Bengali household upstairs had left for Calcutta that morning, so he did not hear the footsteps nor the muffled voices or the running water and sometimes even the flushing of the toilet. Ramesh sat in stilled silence inside his skin. Dinner would be a cup of tea, some sel rotis and the peda, his favourite sweet dish.

Movement outside of his window broke the stillness. He saw little feet and giggles. In the shadows, Ramesh could make out that there were at least four to five girls and that they were dressed in saris. He could see sandals huddled together and whispers like they were conferring about something amongst themselves. Their footsteps felt light and happy, carefree and honest. He smiled and watched the movement of the six pairs of feet, the littlest feet was closest to the largest one; the other four were shifting from one position to the other. Then, those footsteps all shuffled downhill and out of his window screen.

Ramesh squatted down to fish out the kettle from under the bead, to boil some water for tea.

As he was pouring water from the canister into the kettle, through his slightly ajar door he surprisingly heard loud and clear the song 'Bhailini aayo . . . agana . . .' which stupefied him to such an extent that the canister almost slipped from his hand. He froze in disbelief. He had wished and waited for forty-three years and had given up. Could it be that there was an actual Bhailini at his doorstep?

He quickly washed his hands and his face, dried them, glanced at himself in his shaving mirror at the foot of his bed and went to receive his guests. Tears glistened in his eyes, his heart brimming with unbounded joy.

He opened the door to magic and technically his first Diwali night here. All the little girls were dressed in red saris, and instead of blouses, they wore long-sleeved T-shirts, and vibrant green necklaces which pulled their outfits together.

Out of the six, three were the Police Babu's daughters, one was the Tibetan magistrate's daughter, one was the professor's daughter, who lived next door to the magistrate, and the littlest one was the neighbourhood Brahmin's daughter. Awestruck and nervous, he let them in and asked them to sit on his bed.

* * *

Wholehearted singing began—the entire Bhailini song. The leader had a piece of paper with the lyrics on it and all of them huddled over the note and sang intently.

All forty-three years that he had lived in this town culminated in this single moment of exuberance. His smile was brighter than all the diyas put together that night.

He clapped his hands ceremoniously. He laughed with them when they had to reduce the number of dancers from the choreographed song due to limited space. He hummed the Nepali folk song that he had heard while cleaning people's homes, in their radios or their fancy record players. Ramesh watched each child with devotion and admiration.

The Police Babu's daughters sang an English song and the little one danced to a popular Nepali song, directed by the magistrate's daughter.

When they were done singing and dancing, he offered them pedas and sel rotis. He had observed that money was given as a gift to these singing, blessing groups. On a plate, he placed one of the diyas and the Rs 10, assorted in all one-rupee notes.

The Brahmin's daughter ate the peda, reaching over for more with her pudgy little hands, wearing the brightest 'lipsticked' smile on her face.

They took the money and stuffed it inside a colourful drawstring cloth purse, sang a beautiful song of blessing and folding their hands in namaste left him in his joy-filled space.

Ramesh felt like he had leaped across to a different land, where for an instant there was no discrimination, prejudice or intolerance. His kettle started whistling and he made his tea. A certain peace settled deep down in his heart as he chewed the sel rotis, after dunking and softening them in the sweetness of his tea.

She had looked straight into his eyes and had said, 'I know you talk about "desh . . . desh" a lot, but your heart is here. You tell me you want to go die in your desh, but then you never make the effort to go there. *Bas*, this is your home.'

'Yes, Sabitri. This is our home now.'

Her voice trailed away in his heart and he slept to the sound of the temple bells and the chanting of the pundit, blessing the valley and had miraculously reached his tiny abode.

Knotted Ties

Tarawengkal, the Shattered Tile

Niduparas Erlang

translated by Annie Tucker
First published in Indonesian.

The *tarawengkal*, or shard of tile, was about the size of the bottom of a small drinking glass and already looked like the embers of the rambutan wood he was using to heat it up—bright red, like a ripe chilli pepper on the tree. But Durahim kept on turning it over and over with a pair of tongs he had made from a split palm frond, the same kind he used when baking shrimp paste to make sambal. Ah, spicy sambal. Durahim had not eaten sambal with his food in almost a week. It was flavourless that way, but what could he do? He still gathered all the different *lalapan*—vegetables and fresh herbs like lemon basil, fireweed, plum mango leaves, the dogfruit or Chinese stink beans which he harvested from the orchard—quite easily; all he had to do was climb up the trees and pick them. But chilli peppers? Oh my, Durahim's crotch grew more painful and sore just thinking about them, and it was even worse when he imagined smearing a bunch of chilli peppers around his groin. It would smart and burn with a pain that perhaps felt much like the pain of the *anyeng-anyengan* that he was suffering from, and was now trying to treat.

It was not quite ready, he thought. And of course, even though he was using the same palm-frond tongs he used for cooking, that smouldering tarawengkal did not give off the savoury aroma of baking shrimp paste or roasting salt fish, which usually enticed him to hurry and snatch them up, off the fire, or out of the brick oven, as soon as he could.

This time, Durahim did not rush even though, for a while now, the bursts of smoke had been billowing and rolling and had stung his eyes more than once. It felt almost as if the point of a sharp knife had been held near his eyeballs and he had been forbidden to blink his wrinkled eyelids, or the juices of a chilli pepper had been sprinkled on his eyes. For some reason, he felt the smoke from burning, dried, coconut fronds, rambutan wood and coconut husk always stung worse than his plump and gaudily dressed wife's requests for a divorce, although they all repeatedly stung him. More recently, he had been suffering from anyeng-anyengan, which made it difficult for him to sleep. Ah, let his eyes turn red, maybe then his wife would stop haranguing him about this damn sickness—a sickness that had come at the wrong time and place, he thought. Or maybe he should indulge his wife in their rickety bed when his kids went out to evening prayer recitation.

Yes, ever since last night, Durahim had been experiencing excruciating pain in his hips and his groin. It was hot. Irritated. Sore. Severe. It was as if there was a heap of invisible rocks crushing him, thousands of needles stabbing him in the groin from the inside, to the point that he whimpered every time he had to pee, his genitals stinging and burning when the liquid was forced to roll down and drip out. Even just a few drops made him hurt all over.

Soon, the urge to pee once again came to visit, along with more pain in his groin, so he quickly pinched the tarawengkal with his tongs and took it out of the oven, hoping it was ready. Ah, it was completely heated through and had turned an enchanting red, as if it had been long-stewing in the depths of a tranquil hell. He picked up the tarawengkal and felt its heat begin to spread to the tongs and to his myopic eyeballs. He looked at it for a moment, sizing it up. Enough, he murmured, and then he finally placed it down on the dry, cracked earth, a little to the left of the oven. And then, Durahim hurriedly rolled up his sarong and stood straddling the smouldering tile. His body tensed. He flung his head backwards at the pain in his hips and groin. From his laboured expression, it appeared like he was straining to squeeze out his urine while enduring the heat both inside his body and wafting up from below, which felt like it was burning the skin of his thighs.

Durahim strained as hard as death yanking a life, as powerfully as a soul writhing free from a body; he strained like a pregnant woman in the throes of labour—but of course, it was not a baby he was going to deliver. A few moments later, a hiss came from beneath his sarong, like the sound of a freshly forged dagger being dipped into a tub of water. Durahim trembled like a goat caught in the rain with a feeling of satisfaction and happiness. A calm rippled across his face. Ah, was it true that peeing on a smouldering tarawengkal would effectively heal anyeng-anyengan? Moving back a few steps, Durahim hoped that it was true.

But suddenly his expression turned cloudy, gloomy. His eyeballs throbbed when he saw that some blood had leaked down on to and around the tarawengkal. It was not urine—or maybe it was urine mixed with fresh blood. And on top of the tarawengkal, which was no longer smouldering, just slightly off-centre was a white pellet about as big as a soybean. It was not a perfect oval but looked like something squishy about to split open. Oh lord! Now Durahim knew for sure what had been causing him such pain, forcing him to endure such a severe sore heat stinging in his crotch all night long.

* * *

'Dur, Durahim . . . loan me your axe.'

Juhro—a young man who was active in the local youth organization—was shouting for him and banging on the kitchen door. Wearily and a bit lazily, without rancour at the rude summons, Durahim went to the door, the bottom part of which was rotted away, eaten by termites. He turned the latch and pulled the door handle.

The creaking scrape of the door made his teeth ache. 'What do you want to chop down, Juh?'

'Kajali died, Dur. He fell from the dogfruit tree,' Juhro said.

Innalillahi wa innaillaihi rojiun (we come from God and to God we shall return) . . . Durahim was dazed and stunned, filled with disbelief at the shocking and unexpected news. Indeed, who would have expected that death, which was invisible, would drive out Kajali from his native village so quickly? Just yesterday afternoon, he had looked fit and healthy, going around selling eggplant and dogfruit, yelling, '*Saenah . . . nya sae nya ngenah . . .* good and delicious!' That was Kajali's special cry whenever he was selling the harvest from his garden. It didn't matter what he was selling—long beans, eggplant, dogfruit, corn or stink bean—he always called out the same phrase: '*Saenah . . . nya sae nya ngenah,* good and delicious!' Kajali's voice rang in Durahim's ears, but of course, this time the voice was coming from inside his own head, because Kajali would never call out again.

Durahim was subdued for a few moments, either because of the pain in his groin or his grief over Kajali's death, but then he got a grip of himself. Clutching his lower back like an old arthritic man, Durahim picked up the axe that lay on the woven bamboo container in the corner of the kitchen by the water jug. He gave the axe to Juhro, 'I'll join you in a moment.'

And that was how, in this village, when one of the villagers left on a long journey—taken by death—all of the men, young and old, would flock to the house of the deceased, bringing an axe or a machete. They would chop down a tree, chop down bamboo, chop down a banana stalk, gather dry branches, cut off dry palm fronds and split firewood. The pile of firewood was not to cremate the deceased but to carry on the tradition of *tahlilan*. For a week, people would read the Al Quran and pray for mercy on the soul of the deceased. Meanwhile the women—including Durahim's wife, who always looked coquettish with her face covered in thick powder and her lips daubed with red lipstick, whether she was going to someone's wedding or a funeral—also hurried to the house of the deceased carrying shiny knives. A few of them also brought basins filled with a litre or two of rice. *Syahdan*, the death ritual, had to be celebrated in this way. Sometimes, it was even more festive than the wedding of a headman's son, which featured sexy *jaipongan* and *dangdutan* singers and dancers. The mourning family, which was torn apart, plagued by the deep suffering, had to greet the neighbours as they arrived. They had to prepare coffee and tea in large pots, pour sugar into jars and put clove cigarettes into glasses for the men who were chopping wood, digging the grave and fashioning the bamboo casket, as an offering and perhaps also a way of saying thank you.

Juhro, who swayed under the axe he was carrying on his right shoulder, was greeted with a mahogany stump about three feet long as soon as he arrived at Kajali's house. Quite a number of men were already there, splitting wood, making the casket and the bier to wash the corpse.

'Start chopping right away, Juh,' said Mardi, the head of the village council and also the head of the local youth organization, from where he was sitting, taking a break and smoking.

'Yes, sir,' he nodded. Juhro stripped off his shirt, exposing his narrow chest. Flexing his arm muscles, he raised the axe high over his head and swung it as hard as he could. The wounded wood did not completely split but let out a loud crack that hung in the hot midday air. Juhro repeated the same movement, while he perspired profusely and the thick hair in his armpits emitted a funk. Ah, the smell of this sweat, the smell of this fold of flesh was what Durahim's wife liked, so much so that she had asked for a divorce a number of times. But who else would care about Juhro's body odour on a day as hot as this? The other men, who were also busy chopping, were probably thinking more about the smell of their own armpits and their own sweat, which taken altogether was much acrider than the stink of Juhro's armpits.

After a few swings and pounds of the axe, the mahogany stump, as wide around the girth as a grown man, cracked and split. Juhro seemed satisfied and his smile launched, went flying and crashed into the cheeks of Durahim's wife as she passed by carrying a knife. Their eyes met. Oh my, they were like young teenagers, throwing and catching smiles that bloomed like flowers.

* * *

Frigid night. A sombre yet spirited atmosphere had settled over Kajali's house. Voices that had been hurriedly reciting the 'Surah Ya Sin', to proclaim God's sovereignty and the truth of resurrection, were now reciting clamorous prayers. The crowd filled the house to overflowing and spilled out on to the front terrace, absorbed in their chorus of chants and amens. On the edge of the terrace, under the soft yellow light of a 10-watt bulb, peaceful and dim, Durahim stood grimacing, enduring the pain in his crotch and the weight in his hips. His right hand stopped massaging his lower back for a moment to reach out and poke Mardi, who was sitting down next to him.

'I'm going home. My anyeng-anyengan is acting up again,' he whispered, while his other hand plucked a few clove cigarettes from the glass and slipped them into the folds of his sarong. Mardi just nodded slightly.

Durahim shuffled away, looking for his flip-flops in the clutter of all the other flip-flops and sandals that lay in a messy pile. Overwhelmed by the sheer effort of looking for them, or because he couldn't stand the pain any longer, he slipped on a random pair, rolled up his sarong to his knees and hurried away without further ado. He could have peed under a palm tree or a banana tree, as he usually did whenever he was in the orchard, but on a night like this, when someone had just died—what's more, when the deceased was his own neighbour—he felt that it would be sacrilegious to pee just anywhere.

Arriving in front of his dilapidated stilt house, panting and gasping for breath, Durahim heard his wife sighing and moaning, and a voice whispering softly from inside the bedroom. There were also a few creaks from the divan. Ah, maybe his child hadn't yet come home from the neighbourhood mosque or was watching television at a neighbour's house. By this time, all the married men in the neighbourhood had left to participate in the funerary tahlilan, so none of them would dare come out of their houses, not after someone had died. Ugh, those sounds were ludicrous, but they were also infuriating. Durahim trembled with rage, and his anyeng-anyengan flared with a wrenching pain, carving him up from the inside.

He picked up a rock that was twice as large as his fist. He tested its heft in his hand, and then hurled it on to the roof. There was the crash of breaking and splintering tiles. A few of them crashed down and put a stop to his wife's moans and sighs which were heartbreaking and humiliating to him. A perfect silence fell over the night. Now Durahim would have plenty of tarawengkal to turn into smouldering embers and piss on.

Serang, 6 January–4 February 2011

The Peanut Turtle

Dennis Yeo

We were on our way home. This was our first family trip to Malaysia. I had never travelled out of Singapore before. I took the ferry to St John's Island last year but that didn't count. We had gone to Segamat. My papa grew up in Segamat when he was a small boy. We went there to celebrate his god's birthday. There was a big house and all my uncles, aunts and cousins were there. I didn't know many of them as I had never seen them before. I also met my grandmother—Papa's mummy. She tried to speak to me in Hokkien. I couldn't understand what she was trying to say, so I ran off to play with my cousins. We left in the morning, but we would only reach Singapore at night. The road had only one lane. There was nothing to see but rubber trees and palm oil trees. The rubber trees stood like sentinels in straight rows. I didn't know that oil came from trees that looked like pineapples. The road was serpentine, winding left then right then left again. My *kor kor*, *jie jie* and I swayed from side to side, pretending we were on a roller coaster. We were in a row of cars that were all stuck behind a lorry. The driver of the first car had to stick his head out, to make sure that there were no cars coming down in our direction and quickly overtake the lorry. There were cars zooming past us from the other direction too. It was quite dangerous. Papa's old Morris Minor couldn't go very fast and there were five of us in it, so it was quite heavy. In the trunk was the first thing I had ever won in my life—a huge turtle made of peanut candy. I won the turtle just by throwing two stones on the floor. They also gave me a yellow triangle. Mummy told me that I had to bring it with me when I went to school as it would protect me. It was in my mummy's handbag because she was afraid I would lose it. I leaned my head against the window. It was always exciting at first. I wanted to see everything but after a while, it was just the same thing over and over again. Kor Kor and Jie Jie were singing along with the radio, but I was counting rubber trees and after a while, fell asleep.

As I recalled the trip I had made as a child, I thought about how it must have been for my dad to have made that same trip when he was a teenager to settle in Singapore. It was 1957 and he was nineteen. At the time, the Chinese in Malaysia were not given the same opportunities and benefits as the Malays, so he decided to take a chance and get a job in Singapore. With only seventy ringgits in his pocket, he hitched a lift on a lorry driven by a family friend down the very same road we must have taken. In the same way, my grandfather had made an even more perilous journey from Fujian province to Segamat in 1914. The hardware business my grandfather started is still there today. With the money he made, he bought some land and

built a house for his family in 1928. Dad was the third son
of his third wife, who bore him eleven children. My dad
was the first of his family to move to Singapore, paving the
way for two younger brothers to join him later. His other
brothers are now scattered across Malaysia and the globe.
He had done well for himself; married Mum, had us, had
grandkids, bought property and lived a full and contented
life. Having survived the Second World War, economic
downturns and COVID-19, it was poignant to see him
here now in a hospital bed, fighting for each breath. His
smoking habit had finally caught up with him.

When my grandfather left China, he brought with
him a six-inch tall figurine of a deity called Bao Sheng Da
Di. It is believed that this deity was once an actual human
named Wu Ben Hua, who was worshipped by the locals
after his death. Wu was born in 979 AD. According to
legend, his mother dreamt of swallowing a white turtle,
and discovered that she was pregnant when she woke up.
When Wu was born, the room was filled with a heavenly
fragrance and bright colours. His mother had a vision of
heavenly messengers escorting a divine boy down to earth to
become her baby. Wu grew up to be an intelligent boy with
an amazing memory. He became a famous healer, treating
the poor and exorcizing evil spirits. Historical records say
he cured the mother of an emperor of the Song Dynasty.
Folklore claims he once removed a foreign object from a
tiger's throat and even applied eyedrops to a dragon's eye.
Due to his kind acts, he achieved enlightenment, but instead
of entering nirvana, he chose to stay in the mortal world in
seclusion as a shaman on the Mount of Great Wild Goose.
When he died in 1036, it is said he ascended to heaven on
a white crane. People from Fujian began to pray to him

for good health and protection. In 1425, Wu was granted a deified status by an emperor in the Ming Dynasty and conferred the title of imperial inspector of heavenly gate, miracle doctor of compassion relief, great Taoist immortal, and the long-lived, unbounded, life protection emperor (which is Bao Sheng Da Di in Mandarin).

We reached Ayer Hitam. Mummy woke me up. It meant we were halfway home. It was past lunchtime. We had stopped here for lunch on our way to Segamat as well. Papa told me that 'Ayer Hitam' was Malay for 'Black Water'. Like the animals in Africa that stopped at watering holes, people stopped here as they travelled up and down Malaysia. While we were asleep in the car, we didn't feel like 'shee-sheeing', but now that we were up, we all needed to shee-shee. Kor Kor stayed awake so he had to shee-shee on the way to Ayer Hitam. Papa had to stop by the roadside. Mummy told us that every time we shee-shee in the outdoors, we have to whisper to the spirits who might be there to go away otherwise we would inadvertently shee-shee on them and they would get angry. The toilets in Malaysia were very dirty and stinky. Mummy applied tiger balm under our noses so that it wasn't quite so smelly. I held my breath and quickly 'shee-sheed' so that I could get out quickly. It was just a hole in the ground, and I was afraid I would fall in and get swallowed up whole. I didn't dare touch the walls and the flush did not work. Nothing worked in Malaysia. Even the people didn't work. They just sat around all day, talked and drank their coffee. When we were in Segamat, they talked all night until the next morning. No one was in a rush to go anywhere. Not like Singapore. Everything was slower in Malaysia. It was like a time machine. We had gone back into the past. No escalators, no shopping malls, no apartments. Just farms, little towns and rubber trees.

It was very different. Even the *wan tan mee* tasted different. Although I was hungry, I didn't finish mine. The gravy was very thick and black. Papa said he missed his Segamat *kway teow*. We sat together at a round table beside the road while he drank his coffee. He didn't like to be rushed. So, we just sat there as he lit a cigarette and made smoke signals like an Indian chief. Before we left, Mummy said we had to shee-shee again.

One by one, our family became Christian except Dad. We hadn't planned it that way. I became a Christian because of a teacher, my brother because of his friends, and my sister because she was in a mission school. An aunt had brought Mum to church. As a newly converted teenager, I unleashed my fervent faith on Dad who was the only stiff-necked pagan who would not see the light and be saved. He considered himself a free thinker.

He believed that, 'All religions teach us how to do good; it does not matter which one you follow.'

I considered him a coward who would not commit himself to a particular belief system. To him, Taoism, Buddhism, Confucianism and ancestral worship didn't believe in the concept of God, so he subscribed to the idea of self-development and karma as a means of finding contentment, happiness and peace.

'What is good, we absorb,' he said. To me, that didn't solve the issue of an afterlife. I had been taught that my belief answered the fundamental three questions: Where do I come from? What am I doing here? Where am I going? Everyone was on a journey with a destination. Without faith, any significance would decompose into nothingness. Would it matter what rites and rituals were performed at his funeral if it would not affect eternity?

It was only much later that I realized why Dad would find it difficult to believe in what he considered a western god.

When the family house in Segamat was built in 1928, the altar for Bao Sheng Da Di was placed in the central hall of the house. At the altar, there was a miniature sedan chair with four legs, the size of a stool. When someone was facing a problem or was sick, he could pray to request the presence of the deity. Two bearers would then pick up the chair, each holding on to two legs of the chair. They knew the deity had arrived when they felt a palpable weight on the chair, which would begin to rock and move on its own. The deity responded by banging on a table with the chair, scribbling in some unknown language on the tabletop or on a talisman with one of the legs. One of the chair bearers was specially appointed by the deity to interpret these messages. The chair would remain motionless if this bearer was absent. After the advice, or medicinal prescription, was given, the sedan chair would suddenly stop moving, signalling that the deity had left. At times, the deity became angry when devotees did not heed his advice and returned again with the same problem. For instance, a devotee who consulted the deity was told to wind up his business. He refused and lost everything. News of the presence of the deity in the house spread and devotees would flock here for consultation and worship.

We were near Johor Bahru. People called it JB. I knew we were approaching Singapore because there were more cars with Singapore licence plates. I was happy that there were more people now and fewer rubber trees. Singapore was a city with tall buildings and Malaysia was like our countryside but with jungles. In the past, Singapore was part of Malaysia, then they kicked us out, but now we are better. We stayed in a three-room flat in Queenstown. It had two rooms and one hall. It was called 'Queen's Town' because of the British Queen. It was the first housing estate in Singapore. Before that, it was swamps and farms. There was also a graveyard and a British army camp. Luckily the graveyard was on the Holland Road side. We stayed at *zhup lak lao*. Tell any taxi driver 'zhup lak lao' and he would know where to go. At the end of Commonwealth Close, there are three sixteen-storey flats on top of the hill. Papa took me up there once. It was so high, I didn't dare to look down. I could see Mandarin Hotel from there. Zhup lak lao was famous because they were the tallest flats at that time and people who wanted to jump to their deaths went there. Papa said it was called 'Lovers' Leap'. I didn't know what he meant.

I watched the slow rise and fall of Dad's chest, fearful that his final breath would render it motionless. The steady beep of the heart monitor assured me of a sign of life. Everyone dies; it was just a matter of when and how. I knew that my heart too was a ticking time-bomb that would one day be the death of me. My dad's mother, my grandmother, had died of a cardiac arrest. His eldest brother had been sitting in the middle of the rubber plantation he loved when he too had suffered a heart attack. I had thought that that would be the way Dad would go too. Mum began having dementia and became increasingly lost in her own world. Being incarcerated with her during the circuit-breaker period imposed by the government during the COVID-19 pandemic had tested his patience. Her tantrums had driven Dad back to the hypnotic calm of tobacco, which he had tried many times to quit for his children. Mum's frustration was understandable. Who do we become when we lose our memory? Who gets to tell our story? I was prepared for my heart to stop but I was reluctant to part with my brain.

My father was about seven years old when the threat of a Japanese invasion of Malaysia loomed. At first, my grandfather and his brothers intended to evacuate their families to Muar but when they asked the deity for confirmation, they were advised to flee to the third uncle's estate at Bukit Siput instead. Later, it was learnt that the Japanese had killed the Chinese in Muar. The family built a settlement deep into the estate to avoid the Japanese. The dwellings stood on stilts to protect themselves from wildlife and they dug underground tunnels to hide in. The deity told my grandfather to build a hut halfway up a hill. The higher ground provided a vantage point to watch the roads and surrounding paddy fields that the Japanese had to cross to reach them.

A Japanese army officer and his retinue once ventured across the muddy lowlands. The older children who were on guard raised the alarm to pack up and escape deeper into the jungle, leaving my grandfather alone to face the Japanese. When the soldiers arrived, my grandfather welcomed them and made some Ovaltine to show his hospitality. The officer was suspicious and asked for an empty cup. He poured some of the beverage out and ordered my grandfather to drink it before he drank from his cup. Looking at the photographs around the house, the officer asked my grandfather in broken Mandarin where all the kuniang were. My grandfather pretended he did not understand what he was saying. After the Japanese left, the family took down all the pictures of the women in the household, put them in bags and buried them behind the house.

This was the first encounter that the family had with the Japanese. The family stayed in the estate undiscovered for six months feeding on tapioca and sweet potato. The family believed they were protected from snakes and tigers by the deity. After most of the Japanese army had advanced further south, the deity set a date for them to emerge from the jungle and return to their home in Segamat. The deity told the women to cut their hair and don men's trousers so they would look less appealing. The family house was undamaged, but the Japanese had turned a residence nearby into officers' quarters. Again, this turned out to be a blessing in disguise. The presence of Japanese officers ensured that any dishonourable soldier seeking female company would stay away from the vicinity. Being neighbours with the Japanese also benefited the family in other ways. The Japanese would give the innards and trotters to the family when a pig was slaughtered for their dinner as these did not suit their palate. The deity thus protected the family until the Japanese retreated.

We were not that far away. We had been in the jam for more than an hour, inching forward like a snail. Cars, lorries and buses were all 'horning'. The motorcycles whizzed right past. Some people got so fed up that they got off the bus and walked. We could see Singapore from Malaysia. All we had to do was cross the bridge to get to the other side. Mummy held our five red passports open, and Papa handed them over to the customs officer. Like library books, they were 'chopped' and then we were free, with blue water and sky on both our left and our right. It felt funny to be on the Causeway. We were not in Malaysia and we were not in Singapore. We were not anywhere. We were in the middle. The windows were wound down so we could feel the wind. On our left were huge pipes for the water that Singapore bought from Malaysia. During the Second World War, the British said

Singapore was their fortress. They bombed the Causeway to stop the Japanese from crossing over but, in the bargain, they also bombed the pipes, so Singapore had no water. Singapore had nothing. The Japanese just wanted to conquer it to show the British that they could win. 'Welcome to Singapore' the sign read. It was good to be back.

It was dusk. My siblings would be arriving soon to relieve me of my watch. I traced the silhouette of Dad's wrinkled and weathered face in the looming darkness. Dad and his younger brother had been struck by measles when he was five. His brother had died from an overdose of aspirin which was all they had then. The left side of Dad's body was weakened but he had survived. If he had died, I would not be here. What entity decides who dies and who lives on to give life? My siblings and I were given our names by the deity. Dad had made trunk calls back to Segamat when each of us was born, to ask for the deity to be consulted on what to name us, and he had carved our names into the table. Even though Dad had left Segamat, his belief in the deity remained strong and he would faithfully go back annually to celebrate the deity's birthday. Would this deity not heal my father now?

Family members come home to Segamat from all over the world for the birthday celebration of the deity. A week before the festivities, the deity draws up a guest list of spirits he wants to invite. This may include Buddha, Kuan Yin, other deities and Chinese generals from the past. He also decides the number of tables and how much food is needed for the party. There is even a seating plan. For instance, the sun god has the best seat because he is the most powerful because nothing can live without the sun. The food offerings are served on, what may appear to us, empty tables. The deity will go from table to table on his sedan chair to welcome his guests, instructing his devotees to pour tea or liquor for his invisible guests. The more uncouth soldiers are reputed to enjoy brandy and whiskey and tend to be big eaters. An opera puppet show is also performed to entertain these spiritual guests. After the guests leave, prayers are offered before devotees feast on the food. At the end of this mystical evening, reconnected friends and relatives part ways and return to their own lives, hoping that their paths will converge again the following year.

On the night before we left, there was a huge crowd around the altar in the hall. I remember seeing something strange—two men were holding what looked like a chair and swinging it through the air and hitting it on the surface of a table. My cousins and I were in the next room, playing, when I heard my name being called. I was pushed to the front of the altar and made to kneel before it. Two smooth pieces of wood were given to me. They were straight on one side and curved on the other, like two crescent moons. Everyone was speaking in Hokkien, so I didn't know what was happening. Mummy was beside me and she told me to throw the stones on the floor so I threw them down. When I did, everyone suddenly started laughing and cheering. I had won the top prize in a lucky draw and won the peanut turtle.

We got home, tired and hungry. Papa put the turtle on the dining table. It was huge and sat on a wooden plank, colourfully decorated and wrapped in clear plastic. He told me the turtle meant that I would be blessed with a long life. I couldn't wait to eat it so I asked if I could take a bite. It was my prize after all. He used his strength to break off a piece as it was rock-hard and made of sugar-candy and peanut. When I took my first bite of the turtle, one of my baby teeth fell out.

The Broken Window

S.P. Singh

Thirteen hours of backbreaking journey had brought him to the New Delhi Airport. He had flown over one ocean and two continents and landed in the third. Most of the passengers—a mixed group—had slept during the flight. However, his co-passenger, a young man in his thirties, had stayed awake throughout. The brief interaction with him had been uninspiring. When the young man immersed himself in his iPad, he closed his eyes and chose to walk down memory lane, running into twenty long years. In his mind the images of his native village moved faster than his heart could digest. It was difficult to keep pace with his memories.

Twenty years ago, as an undergraduate, he had come to the United States to do his master's degree in civil engineering. He was one of the lucky few chosen for the scholarship by an institute in the USA. A sense of bewilderment had struck him when he had landed at JFK International Airport. A village boy from a backward region in central India had entered El Dorado. It was a kind of a fairytale journey about which thousands of Indian youth dreamed each year but only a couple of hundreds realized.

For two years, he toiled hard to achieve the top honours in the master's degree. As his father couldn't afford his expenses, he did odd jobs to meet them. During the campus placement, a reputed company offered him a well-paying job, which he could not refuse and thus, he made an alien land his second home. The memories of his homeland slowly folded up into nostalgia. A year later, he met Meira, a Mexican who worked in the same company. They fell in love and after a year of courtship, married, riding roughshod over differences in religion and culture. Meira came from a large family, half of which lived in a small town eighty miles east of Mexico City and the other half lived scattered over a dozen cities in the States. He had met his in-laws at the marriage. Would he ever be able to meet Meira's large family? He wasn't sure.

Back home in India, his relatives remembered him at their convenience. He had left behind hardly any friends. Once in a while, his brothers telephoned him to ask if he intended to return to India. When they heard that he had settled down in the United States permanently, they breathed a sigh of relief. Thereafter, their tone became polite, and they invited his family to come and spend their summer holidays in the village. Their talks often centred on the financial difficulties they faced and asked him if he could send them some money. But not even as a formality did they ever ask about the life he now led. Those few minutes were his life's most tormenting moments. Mercifully, his brothers called him only twice a year.

A broken destiny he inherited, a broken destiny he lived.

Carrying the burden of broken dreams and a heavy heart, he alighted the plane. As he completed the immigration formalities, it suddenly occurred to him that he had an official name that had faded into memory as soon as he moved ahead. To get rid of the mild headache, he walked into the cafeteria and ordered a cappuccino. It gave some respite to his aching limbs but little comfort to his troubled mind. His village was miles away and he had to undertake several journeys to reach there.

As he passed through the exit, he walked past several taxis. Some drivers chose to ignore a middle-class Indian passenger, while the others showed no interest at all, probably fearing haggling. A few taxis away, he found a disinterested driver.

'Will you take me to the Railway Station?'

'Which one, sahib?'

'New Delhi.'

The driver picked up his suitcase and dumped it into the boot. Closing the door, he asked, 'Sahib, have you come to visit the Taj Mahal?'

'Why?

'You're travelling light.'

'Oh,' he smiled. 'I'm on an urgent visit. My mother is sick.'

The driver continued, 'I've heard there are no poor people in America. Even sweepers and maids drive cars to work. My acquaintance, a taxi driver, came to India last year and told us that he lived in a huge bungalow there and earned more than an IAS officer.'

He smiled at the man's simplicity. The taxi driver was not the only one mesmerized by those myths. Almost every Indian believed that America was like heaven and nursed a dream to live there someday.

'Passengers coming from abroad carry large suitcases with gifts for their family,' the driver continued.

'You're right,' he said, looking at the man, 'but I'm here to visit my ailing mother.' He wished his positive choice of words could change the condition of his mother who actually was on her deathbed.

It made the driver fall silent for a while.

Five years ago, his mother had visited him in San Antonio. Initial inhibitions had kept him on tenterhooks. He had feared that a meeting between the two most important women in his life might raise a storm in the house. With bated breath, he waited for the fireworks but to his utter surprise, his mother gave his wife a warm, long hug. Perhaps the name, Meira, and her looks did the trick. With her behaviour, Meira straightway warmed her way into his mother's heart. In the old woman's mind, a foreign woman was 'white-skinned' and bereft of culture. But Meira had broken that myth. Like a typical Indian *bahu*, she had touched his mother's feet and had ushered her into the house in the traditional Indian style. It surprised him too. It occurred to him that Meira was friends with a few Indian women in the neighbourhood.

In the very first week itself, Meira won his mother's heart with her broken Hindi. One night, his mother winked at him and said, '*Munna*, my bahu will speak better Hindi than I do before I leave.' Thereafter, she diligently started teaching Meira Hindi. Their after-dinner Hindi classes were the funniest moments of his life. The women learnt less and laughed more. He had never found his mother so happy after his father's death. He was surprised at the way they had developed a strong bond with so much ease and in so little time.

In the evenings, when he chatted with his mother alone, she heaped praises on Meira, drawing comparisons to her Indian daughters-in-law. It made him proud that his Mexican wife had won the title of the best bahu.

For the three months that his mother stayed with him, Meira was extra polite with him. Almost every day he had to call up his brothers with whom his mother chatted and gleefully told them that her Munna, her pet name for him, lived like a king in America. With every call, the list of demand for goodies, mobile phones, laptops, clothes, etc., increased. She proudly told them that her Munna would buy her everything.

Meira and he had saved to fulfil his family's demands so that her mother could return home with her head held high. He had often insisted that she stayed with them forever and he would have her documents done, but she refused. She said that she wanted to be cremated in the village where his father rested. When he realized that she would not relent, he gave up. As the day of her departure drew close, both the women talked more and more. Both tried to prepare for the day of parting. That day arrived sooner than they had prayed for. The evening before her departure, his mother called them both to her room and took out an old, gold necklace. Placing it around Meira's neck, she spoke, with tears in her eyes, 'This is my mother's necklace and I'm glad it has found its rightful owner.'

'But, *Amma*, how can I accept this? I'm your youngest daughter-in-law,' Meira protested.

'*Chup*,' she brushed aside her objection. 'Don't you doubt your mother-in-law's judgement.'

She looked at him.

'Munna, next time when you come to India, I want you to bring her along. I'll organize a huge function in her honour and invite the entire village,' she commanded.

He nodded.

Before she left, he hugged Amma for a long time. 'We'll meet soon,' she consoled him. His teary eyes followed her until she vanished in the crowd.

'Sahib, station,' the taxi driver broke into his thoughts.

He paid the fare and walked into the station. An hour later, the train arrived. Perhaps that was his last journey to the village. Unlike the American trains, it was jam packed and smelled of stale food, spilled tea and soft drinks. Some jittery passengers shouted and stepped over one another's feet, looking for their berths. A few of them haggled with coolies before making the payment. Mothers tried to control their naughty kids. Vendors moved around selling tea, coffee, water and other eatables. The pandemonium gave him a headache. Suddenly, the train started moving. People who were there to see their friends and relatives off said a hurried goodbye and jumped out of the train. The cold dinner and hot tea satisfied his hunger. Stretching on the upper berth, he was reminded of his childhood. In the village, his father owned the biggest house that had a large living room, the *baithak*. In the central wall, facing the road was a large window with glass panes, which no other house within fifty miles had. After the servant had cleaned the rooms and windows, his father wiped the panes again with a clean cloth. Then he sat by the window and watched people and animals pass by. He raised his hand and greeted the people. Most folks greeted him back and moved on. A few of them chatted with him for a while before going back to work.

During the British rule in India, in the same baithak, his father held secret meetings with his friends and planned many mini mutinies that never happened. However, he took part in a few rallies of the Azad Hind Fauz. After Independence, he narrated stories from the Ramayana and the Mahabharata to people who cared to listen to him. But he spent most of his time with friends, who left him one by one. Suddenly, he became lonelier and sadder.

Why was Munna his favourite child? His father never told him the secret, but he enjoyed the adulation. Of all the stories he remembered, the one relating to the glass window had a lasting impact on his mind. Many years ago, his father had called the family into the baithak and said, 'Evil spirits exist in the world alongside the human beings, but nobody can see them. They sneak in through broken doors and windows, poison our minds and destroy us. So, to protect our family, we should close the doors and the windows in the night.' And he ensured that someone did that before he went to bed.

In his last few days, it pained his father to see the glass panes develop bubbles and become hazy. He sat by the window and waved at the blurred images passing by the house. Then one day, the unthinkable happened. A storm struck the village at midnight and broke two of its eight panes of glass. When his father woke up in the morning, he found two large holes in his favourite window.

His repeated pleas to repair the broken glass went unheard by his sons for the next few months. It took a hunger strike by him to get the window repaired. His failing health scared his eldest son, who called the carpenter and asked him to replace the broken panes with coarse wooden planks to save money. Every nail that he hammered hurt his father.

The wooden panes blocked the view and hastened his father's demise. In his last moments, Munna was with his father and noticed a deep sadness in his eyes. His father told him that the broken window was a bad omen, and the evil spirits would now freely enter the house and destroy his family. Finally, his father left for his heavenly abode.

Before his mother departed from San Antonio, she urged him to return to the village and repair the broken window. It had hurt him to hear from her that none of his brothers had bothered to repair that. What his mother had hidden from him was that all his brothers ran separate kitchens, and that she cooked her food in hers. Despite living with her three sons, the mother lived a lonely life. Had he known that, he would have prevailed upon her to remain with him. But it was too late.

Burdened by the thoughts, he fell asleep.

The morning brought him one step closer to his village. He alighted from the train and came out of the platform, expecting horse-drawn carriages to be lined up. The sight of autorickshaws came as a pleasant surprise to him. He hailed one. After an hour's journey, he reached his village. Alas! No further surprises awaited him. The parental house, despite some damages, still held its magnificence. The broken window caught his attention. It hurt him to see that the window had suffered further damages. All eight panes of glass were missing. Four of them had been boarded up with wooden planks and the other four had not been repaired.

Soon his nephews and nieces ran out towards him in the hope of getting gifts but were rather disappointed when their Munna *chacha* handed them chocolates that he had picked up at the railway station. Tearing through the restive crowd, he entered the baithak where his mother lay on her bed. He bent down and took her hands in his. The touch brought a sparkle into those old eyes. She kissed his forehead and spoke in a faltering voice, 'Munna, I'm glad that you came. God has listened to my prayers. I wanted to see you for the last time before I close my eyes ...'

Memories of his childhood flooded his mind. With the glass of milk in hand, she would run after him and he, after great persuasion, would take a few sips before scampering out of the house to play with his friends. She would keep shouting after him, but in vain. She had had a very difficult time feeding him and wouldn't eat a morsel herself until he had eaten his meal. When he was ten, he had a high fever for a week. She sponged his body with a wet cloth every few hours and remained by his bed the whole time. She didn't sleep until his fever broke. When he recovered fully, she took him to the temple and prayed. His eyes welled up. He pressed her hands, but they were cold. He let out a loud wail and burst out crying. Tears streamed down his face. It seemed like she had been waiting to see him for one last time.

After his father's death, Mother had become a strong bridge that connected his new homeland with the old one. He was confident that he could return to his native village whenever he felt the urge to eat mangoes from the orchard, sugarcane from the field, hot jaggery from the barn or corn on a winter night. He had hoped to someday show his children the village he was born in and the places where he had played with his friends. That was not possible now. With the bridge gone, all his connections with his old world were snapped forever.

The news of his mother's death flashed across the village. In minutes, people rushed in from every direction. In the melee, he answered some questions, felt several piercing glances and noticed a few sympathetic gazes. After the cremation, the people went home.

In the night, his bed was laid out in the baithak where his father and then his mother had spent their old age. Nobody surrendered their bedroom to him. Suddenly he felt like an outsider, an unwanted guest.

The moonlight through the broken window fell on the bed and kept him awake for a long time. The memories of that home for many years had given him a lot of strength in the alien land, but now the same memories began to torment him. With the passing away of his mother, the village too had shut its doors to him. Had it been a sin to seek a better future in another country? he wondered.

The next morning, he told the family that he would return to America after a couple of days. Hurriedly, *shanti path* was organized the next day. In the evening, at the behest of the eldest brother, they gathered in the baithak.

'Amma told us that Munna lives like a king in *pardes*,' said his first sister-in-law, lifting her veil.

'He hasn't invited any of us to his palace,' complained the second sister-in-law.

'Wish we were as lucky as Munna's wife,' lamented the third sister-in-law.

An admonishing gaze by the eldest brother made all of them pipe down.

Even in the mourning period, the women had no qualms about airing their jealousies. However, his brothers, particularly the eldest, had always loved him and had pampered him in their childhood with his share of sweetmeats as he was the youngest sibling.

In anticipation, he waited.

'Munna, we know you earn well and don't intend to return. Here, we find it hard to make ends meet. The farm labourers have become costly, and agriculture is no longer profitable.' His eldest brother looked at him and hesitated. 'Well . . . I know it may not be the right time to talk about the . . . property but since you're leaving tomorrow, you may like to settle it once and for all.'

'Our children need to go to schools in the town and we need money for this,' said the second brother, as his wife looked on, expecting more from him.

'We, brothers, have decided to divide the land, the house, the barn, the mango orchards and the animals equally between the three of us,' said the third brother in a judge-like tone.

With rapt attention, he listened to those voices. All of them were collectively uprooting him from his roots. So, the decision must have been made a long time ago, but it was only now being conveyed to him. The broken window's sadistic smile drew his attention. Over the years, the evil spirits had entered their home through the broken window and had destroyed his family.

After pondering over it for a few minutes, he signed the papers abdicating his share of the properties. What a price to pay for those childhood sweetmeats, he smiled.

Later, he went around the village and found a carpenter. Standing outside the house, he instructed him to replace the broken window with a new wooden window. The work lasted over an hour. The carpenter was happy to get more than he had asked for.

At dusk, he closed the window and slept peacefully that night. In the morning, he woke up, got ready and took one last look at the new wooden window. Confident that now the evil spirits would not be able to destroy whatever little was left of his father's large family, he left.

Lata

Gaurav Bajpai

One thing that always amazed me about Lata was her insatiable desire to work. I had seen her in the mornings, carrying milk and bread, then in the afternoons, with a load of rice or flour on her head, followed by snacks in the evenings and ice-cream in the nights—running towards her destination before it melted. All this in her green sari with a black border and a maroon blouse.

Her frail figure and her sweaty face, her habit of biting the corner of her sari, to hold the fabric in place over her head. Her perspiring skin and the effete look in her eyes often delineated the summer heat. Her rubber slippers were a size bigger than her foot, slapping on the concrete of the pedestrian footpath and the tiles of the lobby as if heralding her grand entrance even from a distance. Something that made her stand apart from many others like her, who worked in the Highland Greens Township was her affable nature and her always-ready-to-help personality. It was as if she was omnipresent whenever you needed her.

Our two-bedroom apartment in building seven was a modest dwelling. My husband lived with his parents and, as per the customs of the world, I moved in with him post marriage. I had lived in an independent house until my marriage and moving to a high-rise was a new experience for me. That too in a township where you could easily get all your shopping needs met within one compound. There were several shops for all the essentials within the township and I always considered the beauty parlour the cherry on the cake.

Lata used to work in Dolly's Beauty Parlour, one of the many establishments in our township. The parlour served the 350 families in the eight-building complex.

Dolly Aunty, the patron of the beauty parlour, was an effusive lady in her late fifties. I always found her wearing a sleeveless, ankle-length gown, which revealed her flabby arms, coupled with contrasting leggings. Her face looked radiant, with professional-looking makeup that deftly hid her wrinkles. Her hair had a new colour streak every month, a perk of owning a beauty parlour.

'How can you say that she has a different colour every time? I saw her today, and it seemed all the same purple,' said my husband one day when he had chanced upon Dolly Aunty in the township's grocery store.

'It's mauve,' I replied.

'Yes, purple,' he looked at me. I narrowed my eyes.

He smiled and took his usual seat in front of the television without any further discussion. He must have realized that men know only the basic colours—red, blue and green; or the VIBGYOR. For women, there are so many more. Our lives are much more colourful.

It was my first time in the beauty parlour when I met Lata.

'Hi, *beta ji*! How are you? Your MIL called to tell me you would be visiting. Welcome to the township and congratulations on your wedding,' greeted Dolly Aunty from behind her billing desk, which was nearly as tall as her. She extinguished a matchstick and threw it on the ground. A strong smell of sandalwood floated around from the incense burning in the small mandir behind the billing desk. I gave her a surprised look and muttered, 'MIL?'

'Mother-in-law, beta ji!' she exclaimed. I couldn't resist grinning back, at her infectious smile and the acronym.

'My mother-in-law was all praises for the excellent work that your staff did during my wedding,' I told her.

She gestured towards the parlour chair and said, 'Today of all days is a little tough. I have two girls who manage the work here, and both are running late. Also, I have to run to the bank across the street. We'll start with a foot massage. Lata can do it. I'll send her in immediately, and that is complementary!'

She ran out of the door without waiting for me to voice my concerns. I was left inside, staring at her parlour and listening to her fading voice.

When Lata finally entered, I had mixed feelings of shock and anger. I couldn't visualize her as one of the beauticians who would be giving me a foot massage, with her calloused hands and dishevelled appearance. It looked like she had rushed to the parlour as soon as she got the directive from her employer and was huffing from the exertion, wiping the beads of sweat from her forehead using her green saree. She gave me a huge smile and gestured to me to take a seat.

The parlour had three chairs, one of them attached to a sink. The seating required some manoeuvring. I was too dazed at the thought of being attended by such a sloppy-looking beautician that I didn't even try to move the chairs. Lata realized my predicament. She switched on the fan and the air conditioning and quickly came to my rescue, moving the corner seat a bit, making space for me to sit. And then, she swivelled it, making me face her. She handed me some magazines and went about her preparation for the foot massage. I desultorily flipped a few pages of the glossy film magazine but kept an eye on her. I was still not sure how my foot massage would go.

She got the foot massager, plugged it in and pulled up my slacks to my knees. Then she went behind the billing counter and clicked some buttons. A melodious song erupted from the speaker which had been fitted under the glass window, covered with a white, embroidered cloth and crowned with a small flower vase. Lata returned, poured some aromatic oil in her palms and started applying it gently on my legs. Her hands demonstrated some well-practised moves which dimmed my reservations.

'You know, Dolly Aunty did all the makeup for the ladies staying in your house during the marriage. Even your husband got his facial done here,' she giggled. I smiled at her and placed the magazine on the chair next to me.

'How long have you been working here?' I asked.

'Three years. I do the cleaning and cooking work at Dolly Aunty's house and parlour,' she replied, applying the oil on my calves and massaging them.

I looked at her, surprised. So, my inhibitions were justified. She was no parlour staff. Why would Dolly Aunty assign the foot-massage task to a cleaning lady? Why would my mother-in-law not stop raving about the wonderful service that this parlour offered?

'That means you're not trained to do these things,' I said. She sensed me rigidly withdrawing my legs and the tightening of the calf muscles.

'No, don't worry. I have learned this work and I only do foot massage, nothing else,' she smiled, placing my leg on the edge of the massager. She then started kneading my toes.

Some uneasiness crept in and I found myself flinching at her every stroke and squeeze. I started the countdown to end this session and never return. Lata looked at me and saw me cringe, she eased her hands letting my feet rest inside the massager. She stood up and walked over to the wall socket.

'Your mother-in-law had a foot sprain during the wedding preparations. I did the massage for an entire week and now she runs like a horse,' she giggled and switched on the massager.

I found it funny to imagine my mother-in-law galloping like a horse and a smile bloomed across my face.

The massager started whirring with my feet inside it, and I could feel my shoulders drooping as a wave of relaxation washed over me. Lata stood up and washed her hands in the sink. Wiping them on her sari, she reached out for the broom kept in a closet behind the billing counter. It was her second role change in under thirty minutes. She was soon joined by the parlour staff who hurried in as if they had missed their train, but relaxed when they did not find Dolly Aunty behind the billing counter. They dumped their bags in the closet behind the counter and took out their aprons—a pink one with 'Dolly's Beauty Parlour' inscribed in black in the middle.

I too had a similar apron in my new life—responsibilities of cooking and managing the house chores. This was in addition to my hectic working hours. What for me was an apron, was considered a part and parcel of married life by my in-laws and my husband.

'You need to help Mother with cooking,' my husband said, after a week of our being married. I kept the hairbrush on the dresser and turned to look at him.

'She is slightly overwhelmed with the increased workload in the house and can use your help with breakfast,' he continued.

'You know my shift timings. Waking up to fix breakfast might not be possible,' I countered.

'I know but laying out stuff the previous night would also be helpful to her, I suppose. And then, while she cooks breakfast, you can prepare lunch before you leave.'

Stunned, I gaped at him. But I kept my calm and replied, 'Why don't we explore the option of hiring a cook and maid?'

He didn't reply; just walked out of the room to convey those thoughts to his parents.

* * *

'What about your family, Lata?' I asked, as I waited for her to start my massage session after the dramatic discussion with my in-laws about hiring a maid and increasing the expenses; my husband had only been a spectator throughout this.

'My husband is a watchman in the nearby shopping complex. My daughter is six years old and stays with my parents in our village. We send money for her education and food,' she replied. I could see the sparkle in her eyes when she mentioned her daughter. 'This Diwali, I will see her after two years.'

I looked at her, surprised. How can a mother stay from her young child for two years? Lata however seemed impassive about this.

'We talk on the phone every day, and her grandparents keep sending photos of her,' she replied.

An elderly woman peeped into the parlour and asked Lata about Dolly Aunty. She held a dog leash in her hand and

I could hear her pet busily barking at another one crossing the road. I turned to look at her.

'This is Mehta Aunty. She's a regular customer here; comes to get her hair dyed. You will always find her in a red tracksuit with her dog.' Lata whispered to me. 'Her dog bit the secretary of the society last year and since then they have been at loggerheads.'

This was one of the other benefits of a beauty parlour. They were often a reliable source of news about current affairs and other gossip around you. Lata ensured that I was abreast with gossip and rumours floating inside the township, making me an integral part of this extended family.

I tried to give her the best version of my household, including my in-laws and husband; however, things were not falling in the right bucket as I had expected after my marriage.

* * *

I changed my profile and got designated to a different department within the organization, just so that I could move to an office closer to my husband's place. This came with a change in my shift timings, which was taking a toll on my health. And to add to the woes, my involvement in the household chores tired me. My suggestion to employ a maid was turned down unanimously and the reasons cited ranged from security to hygiene, and finally, the added financial strain.

'We want you both to save money and buy a bigger apartment,' my father-in-law reasoned.

'I've been doing all the household chores alone, and can continue, but definitely not a maid,' added my mother-in-law.

I discussed my situation with my mother and she cited examples of compromise that women have long had to make to help sustain their marriage. Left with no choice, I dragged my fatigued self to the kitchen every morning and prepared lunch for my husband and his family. Sometimes, I returned to the room to catch up on my sleep, only to be called back again for laundry or cleaning. My weekends now helped me make up for lost hours of sleep, declining the chances of a movie or dinner date with my husband, and sometimes visiting new relatives with my in-laws. I knew this would be added to the 'grievance' list of my in-laws, but I couldn't get my sleep-deprived brain to worry about the after effects. My new schedule also reduced my parlour visits, and I didn't meet Lata very often.

* * *

'What happened to your eye, Lata?' I asked, looking at the black bruise that covered her right eye, with dried blood still caking around it. I was seeing her after a month and my heart ached to see her like this.

'Nothing, *memsaab* . . . got hurt,' she smiled and tried to cover her eye with her sari. Realizing that she couldn't do it effectively, she turned away and started cleaning out the corners behind the billing counter.

'What do you mean?' I probed.

She continued cleaning the corners, ducking low behind the tables just to avoid having to answer my question. The parlour girl who was doing my root touch-up paused in her task. I saw her reflection in the mirror, looking at Lata, waiting for the answer. It seemed none of the customers had ever paid any heed to the many bruises that Lata carried over the years and none had questioned her about it.

'My husband drinks at times. And yesterday, I think he had a little too much,' she replied, crouching to collect the dust in a dustpan. 'He loves me, though,' she smiled, turning away to the exit and walking out to discard the garbage.

'She's lying! Every day, something or the other happens at her place. Her husband is an alcoholic and takes her money as well,' the parlour girl spoke up. She must have anticipated this evasive answer from Lata and decided to tell me the truth.

'She should inform the police,' I said, irritated.

'Dolly Aunty tried a few times. But her husband gets more violent if he knows that she has been complaining,' the girl replied, dipping the cotton swab in the colour and daubing the roots of my hair.

I wanted to talk to Lata when she came back inside, but I had to hold back when I saw Dolly Aunty enter and take her position behind the billing counter. I didn't see Lata when I got out of the parlour, nor for the next couple of days. Eventually, my woes multiplied in my household as well and I completely forgot about Lata.

* * *

It had been a month since I started doing the household chores along with my work night shifts. The compromise that my mother had asked me to make reflected on my face; exhausted and with red eyes, every morning I would drag myself to the kitchen. It was taking a toll on my health, but the ordeal was not over yet. At the end of the month, on a weekend, my father-in-law called for a meeting. I assumed it was a performance review, but it turned out to be something else.

'Beta ji, I would like you to contribute your entire salary for the house expenses,' he said, leaning forward and crossing his hands on the dining table. My expression was a mix of irritation and surprise.

'Your husband will give you money for your personal expenses,' my mother-in-law added.

I looked at my husband who was nodding and looking at his father.

'We're doing this to manage the household expenses and save for a bigger house, taking into account your future kids' education expenses as well,' he continued.

My husband looked at me and said, 'It's for the family.'

I could feel my face growing hot at this. I could feel the anger and frustration building within me; someone with whom I planned to spend my entire life was crushing my pride and standing on the other side, rather than supporting me.

I couldn't take it any more and with tears welling inside me, I excused myself and walked out of the house.

Staying inside the house was not an option as I knew I would only be dragged into the discussion again. I walked out to the township's garden for some fresh air. My mind was replaying the words that I had just heard—giving my entire salary away and getting what was essentially pocket money for my monthly expenses from my own husband. Was this the twenty-first century? I'm still not allowed to make my own decisions and made to ask permission at every turn; and now, even clip the wings of the bird already in the cage by giving her pocket money every month, from her own salary. I could just imagine how my parent would feel about their independent daughter, being caged by these conjugal obligations. I made a mental note to ask whether my husband was okay with handing over his entire salary, too.

'Excuse me, madam, we need to paint the bench.' A man with his face covered, holding a bucket, was standing over me. I looked up at his paint-splashed undershirt and narrowed my eyes. He pointed to the bench next to mine with the paintbrush in his hand.

The words 'EDUCATE YOUR GIRL CHILD' were painted on the bench in bold.

My eyes were burning with anger, looking at the painted words. They were mocking me, telling me that the society is filled with hypocrites. We never do what we preach. With clenched fists I stood up and then went and sat down under a tree. I could hear my thumping heartbeat and my head throbbed as I watched him, anticipating what he would write next.

'Taking an evening walk, memsaab?'

I looked up and saw Lata smiling down at me. Before I could reply, she sat down beside me.

'You look sad. What happened? Did you fight with *saabji*?' she asked.

'No, just some office pressure,' I replied, trying to avoid her scrutiny, and more importantly, avoid being the next topic of gossip in Dolly's Beauty Parlour.

Lata nodded, 'Working and managing house is very difficult at times,' she said. 'Married life is always a compromise. Especially for girls. We leave our house, move to a new one, adjust to their customs and traditions and still feel like outsiders, adjusting and compromising.'

I looked at her. She was making circles in the mud using a twig. I noticed some new wounds on her hands. Feeling my gaze, she hid them under her sari.

'Is it a form of compromise and adjustment that you have to endure the physical abuse from your husband?' I blurted. It was the pain that I was experiencing and my injured pride that made me say those caustic words and I immediately regretted it. She was still looking down, fidgeting with the twig in her hand. It took her a while to reply.

'You know, memsaab, what the worst thing is about a man hitting a woman? It is at that instant you realize that you're a woman. It doesn't matter how smart you are, or how educated you are. They can use their male force any time to shut you up. It doesn't always have to be their fist, it can be their words as well,' she held my eyes, forcing me to drop my embarrassed gaze towards the man painting the bench.

'MEN AND WOMEN ARE EQUAL'

I looked at the quote in disgust, and then, with disdain, at the man painting it. I turned to look at Lata, but she had already set off towards the beauty parlour. I realized she was carrying a big grocery bag over her shoulders. I hadn't noticed it when she had been sitting beside me. She leaned to one side to counteract the weight of the heavy bag. I followed her with my eyes to the end of the path, until she turned and disappeared inside the parlour.

* * *

'Just imagine how much happier we'd be if you listened to them.' My husband was sitting beside me on the bed, stroking my hair.

'I do listen,' I replied, feeling the lump building inside my throat. 'This is not a question of me giving my salary to them. It is about why I should be expected to—asked to—sacrifice. And this won't stop here. There'll be something else tomorrow and then something more the day after that,' I replied, wiping the tears that just leaked out my eyes.

'You're overthinking it and taking this a little too far,' he said, suddenly standing up and his body tensed as he looked at me. 'Take some time to think about it and we'll discuss this again over the weekend when we go out for dinner,' he said and returned to the living room to watch cricket.

The following week was tense in the house. My husband tried in vain to thaw the ice between my in-laws and me. My anxiety levels rose every day and my resolve dwindled. As I walked out for office on Monday, consumed by my thoughts, I found Lata waiting for me at the township entrance. She waved at me.

'Memsaab, can I ask you something?' she said hesitantly. I nodded.

'Can you lend me Rs 5,000? I want to admit my daughter into an English school. I need to pay the security deposit. I will repay you every month from my salary,' she said, looking down as if anticipating my refusal; it probably had been, by many others, including Dolly Aunty.

Something snapped in me at that instant. My back straightened and I asked her to follow me to the nearby ATM. It was like staking a claim over my freedom. It is my money, and I can give it to anyone I like. I entered the ATM with sure steps and punched in the amount; the whirring of the machine increased my heart rate and I smiled when the crisp currency peeked from inside. I had made the decision and I was proud of that. I gave her the money.

The weeks that followed were the busiest at office. I took some time from my husband to think about our last discussion. I wanted to avoid conflict, although I knew it would resurface again when salary day dawned.

Meanwhile, I visited the parlour twice—once for some small facial job and once for a pedicure—but didn't find Lata. I wanted to ask the parlour staff about her whereabouts but couldn't bring myself to do so. There was this strange feeling of elitism that cropped up every time I tried to ask about Lata. What would they think? Would they wonder why I was asking about her of all people? That was quickly followed by the fear of being ridiculed if they were to discover I had lent Lata money, only to have the woman disappear into the blue.

Eventually, salary day arrived, and I was anticipating the discussion enforced again at the breakfast table. But it didn't come up that morning. I knew this was just the lull before the storm. For the past couple of days, I had been full of self-deprecating feelings. I was working as a finance professional, and my decision to lend money to Lata had fallen flat. I had made the mistake of deciding from my heart, and she had run away with my money.

Was it a good choice to hand over the reins to the elders and let them decide? These doubts engulfed me like dark patches of clouds covering the sun and the light from my life. Wistfully, I made my way out of the house towards my office.

'Memsaab?' A familiar voice called out as I reached the township's gate. I turned to see Lata standing under a tree in her familiar green sari, covering her head. A man was standing beside her, looking in my direction. I could sense the anger rise inside me as I moved towards them, but it evaporated as soon as I saw her bruised head, blood still clotting on the wounds. Her eye was black again and there was a small bald patch on her head, as if someone had grabbed her hair and yanked out a tuft by the roots.

I was aghast, looking at her and imagining what she must have endured over the past few days. My heart shattered to think of the many other bruises that she might be carrying on her frail body, hidden behind her sari. A solitary tear escaped my eye.

'What happened, Lata? Where have you been?' I moved closer and hugged her. She held me tight and a dry sob escaped her throat; the tears inside her had already dried.

'This is Ramesh, memsaab.' She cleared her throat and pointed to the man standing beside her. He folded his hands politely, and I acknowledged the greeting.

'I'm going to my village. He is dropping me off at the railway station.' Her voice shook; maybe because of the trauma she had been through or the physical pain that she was still experiencing.

'And your husband?'

I don't know why I asked this question, but I was glad I did because I could see the rage that had been inside me some time ago, had travelled to Lata's eyes; they were burning red.

'He was arrested today,' replied Ramesh and then looked at Lata.

'I left him for good. There was no compromise this time. Maybe I had been afraid so far, but not any longer. I will live with my daughter and make sure she doesn't have to make any compromise in her life. I will bring her up just like you—independent and confident.' She looked at me with proud, reverent eyes. I was taken aback by her words because I had never thought that someone could look up to me like this or idolize me. Lata had chosen a life similar to mine for her daughter, but in a very different way—she saw education, independence and career for her daughter and that made me happy.

'I came to return the money that I had borrowed from you because I'm going away from here permanently.' She held out a bundle of currency notes which had been secured with a rubber band.

'For your daughter,' I replied, pushing away her hand. 'Teach your daughter to make her own decisions and to never be afraid of anyone.'

Lata broke into a watery smile. I opened my handbag and gave her whatever little money I was carrying. We exchanged phone numbers, a final exchange as we were unsure if we would truly keep in touch or see each other again. I stood there, waving goodbye to her as she walked away. This time, her gait was confident and firm as she went towards her new life—a new beginning.'

My thoughts were interrupted by my mobile phone's ringtone. I saw an unknown number and hesitantly picked it up.

'Good morning, madam. I am calling from Efficient Maid Services. You had done an online enquiry for a cooking maid a few days ago. Are you still interested to know more about the services?' asked the voice at the other end. I looked in the direction of Lata's retreating figure and cleared my throat.

'Yes, I am. Please send the details,' I replied decisively.

It was my turn now to make a decision and do what Lata had just taught me.

An Apartment of Good Intentions

Adriana Nordin Manan

'*Assalamualaikum, Cik*. Are you Hafizah?' the man asked, one foot doing the hearty dig of putting out a cigarette.

'*Waalaikumsalam*, yes. *Encik* Zul? Are you here alone? Didn't your wife come with you?'

'No, sorry. What happened was, I just finished doing a delivery and there were problems, so I finished late. I was worried I wouldn't make it in time here if I went to pick her up before coming. I was afraid you'd be waiting for me . . .'

Hafizah preferred having the wives around. She felt they understood her better and could get on the same page faster than their husbands did. Instead of furrowed eyebrows, there would be earnest nods.

'It's okay. Come.'

Approaching the steps, she took an instinctive sniff, a test to see if she could breathe in normally or had to clip her breaths in case there was a whiff of rotting garbage or a clogged drain or even worse, cat poo.

The neighbours' doors were closed shut, as they always were. The distant murmurs from a television or the occasional clangs of spatula against pan were the only reminders that this was a shared space. The good thing was that, although small, as soon as you entered her place, any outside sounds were bearable, barely noticeable even. Like white noise.

'Where do you live?' asked Zul, as she turned the key.

'My family lives in Setiawangsa. So not far.'

'That's not far at all. Is this place yours or your family's?'

'Mine. But my family helped a bit *lah* . . .' Her reluctance to give up too much information battled her realization that small talk, at the end of the day, was harmless. Plus, she and Zul would be exchanging more nuggets of chatter if things went the way she wanted.

'Good, so young and you already have your own place.'

It was no penthouse, and in the order of living spaces, was a flat. Two steps down from a condo and one down from an apartment, yet comfortably far from being a shack.

But Hafizah had made it homey. There was furniture and a television. The kitchen cabinets were bare, save for a few cups and plates.

Zul tailed Hafizah as they popped their heads into each of the rooms. The master bedroom with the purple-and-blue sheets. The second room with a single bed and study desk. She pictured it being suitable for a teenager or pre-teen. The third room had a bunk bed and curtains with knock-off versions of Mickey and Minnie Mouse in garish colours. Mickey's head looked a bit too bulbous and one of Minnie's ears was bigger than the other.

'This place is very pretty, Cik. My children would like it. My wife too. It's closer to her family. She's from Gombak. From here, it's nearby. We live in Cheras now. It's a bit far.'

He sat on the sofa, ramrod straight without leaning back, like someone who knew he was only passing through.

'Oh, *terima kasih*. That's good that you like it. Do you think you'll take it?'

'How much is the rent again? 700?'

'Yes, but we can talk more about that. Let's go for a drink downstairs and discuss things.' She made a quick sweep of the place to make sure all the windows were closed, and no fans were on.

Zul was giving out the right signals. He kept a good distance when they walked together and didn't ask her for a discount outright like they were negotiating a *pasar malam* transaction of onions or *ikan bilis*.

'Here's the thing, Encik Zul. As I said, the rent is 700. For this area, that's cheap,' she said. He nodded, taking sips of his Nescafe *tarik*.

'It's usually between 800 and 1000. The prices here have gone up. This area, it's now in demand. Plus, my place is furnished.'

He looked at her expectantly, like he was anticipating something good to come out of her hints back at the flat that things were up for negotiation.

'But I'm willing to bring down the rent, if you and your wife are okay to join this programme I've put together.'

'What programme is that? MLM *ke*?'

'No, not MLM. I'm not looking for any down lines or anything like that,' she waved a hand dismissively. 'The programme—calling it a "programme" makes it sound so formal—it's to record how your children are doing in school. You said you have three children, right?'

'Yes. The eldest boy is in Standard Four, and the second, a girl, is in Standard Two. Adik is not in school yet. He's two.'

'That's good. What I'm suggesting is, if your children have good attendance at school and they get good exam results, I'll reduce your rent.'

If Zul was like the others who came before him, there would be a lot of explaining to do. They would ask whether she was a front for some politician. Maybe a welfare department officer. Or someone with less officially conferred authority to be nosy about other people's affairs, but took up the task nonetheless.

She was right. Somewhat.

'Cik, I've never heard of somebody renting out a place with such conditions. Do you work for a *wakil rakyat*?'

She assured him that she was not affiliated to anybody. Throwing in some laughs and banter would convince him more, she figured. She into politics? Tongue click. No.

The signs were promising. Zul did not recoil outright or give the prospective tenant-equivalent of a cat's hiss by becoming defensive or questioning her sincerity.

'This would be good for our family. My children, they like school, although the boy is a bit playful. I think last year he was number twelve in class.'

'That's good. If he gets number one to five, your rent for the following month will be reduced by 100 ringgits. If he and his sister don't miss any days of school, I'll take off fifty for each of them. If they both get good results in the exams and have good attendance, the rent can come down to 400.'

'D'you mean I have to report their attendance to you every month? But the schools here, they don't give out monthly records,' said Zul, with an air of wisdom of someone who knew something and was very happy that he knew it.

'In my time, only if you skipped school for several days would the school report your lack of attendance to your parents.

There was a time when I became a bit of a rascal you know, skipped school, hung out with friends at cyber cafés. My teacher told my father. So, one day, he was waiting for me at home with a belt! But, if you miss a day or two, that's not a problem. You mean, they can't miss even one day, to get this discount?'

The d-word. Hafizah bristled at the mention of it, at the onions and ikan bilis vibe it gave out.

'No, if they're sick or if there's an emergency, then that's fine. I just want to make sure they're serious about school and do well. My intention is just to help.'

'Oh, now I get it. This is something different. I've never heard of it before in my twelve years renting in KL. Tell you what. I'll go home and talk to my wife about it. If she's okay with it, I'll call you, okay Cik?'

Hafizah felt the urge to tell him to ask his wife there and then, but decided against it. She didn't want to sound too aggressive. Feeling the tinge of awkwardness of a petering out conversation, she found herself stirring the spoon in her glass of Milo repeatedly, avoiding any more eye contact than was necessary.

'Okay *lah*, Cik, I'll head home now. I'll have a word with my wife, see what she thinks,' he said, almost on cue.

With a scribble in the air, he called for the bill. She insisted on paying and he was fine with it after his initial demurring that was expected in such situations.

Hafizah hoped that Zul and his wife would take up the offer. When you have something, you want to let go of for a fee, the time between showing it to potential buyers and hearing back from them is the worst. She had learnt that the aftertaste of the first meeting is never the right hint of things to come. There was Rahman with the paunch and receding hairline, who quipped 'this is a great place!' and sang Hafizah's praises, never to be heard from again. And then there was Abang Bob and Kak Wati. They liked the neighbourhood because it was easy to get from there to the many pasar malams where they set up a shop. They seemed interested, but when she followed up, Bob told her that they weren't moving in. There was always that sharp, swift pain of rejection. She felt they never said enough thank-yous for what she was doing and didn't seem sufficiently sorry for not playing ball.

Maybe a better offer came up. Maybe they could never really afford it and were just shopping around. Maybe they did not have the heart to tell her that the place was not really a steal for the price. Maybe they told someone, perhaps a relative that juggled writing noxious comments on social media pages of celebrities and dispensing unsolicited advice to anyone who would lend an ear, who then told them that something sounded fishy, and Hafizah might be up to no good. Maybe the way of life here was to limit the number of people who can make your life a concern of theirs, and with her programme, she was squarely beyond that limit.

The truth was the flat was becoming something that took up more of Hafizah's time than she would have liked. She was twenty-five, intelligent and with passable social skills. She would much rather spend a day out at the movies or hiking, instead of worrying about finding tenants and scheduling viewing sessions. She felt bad about thinking like this because it came into her life thanks to her parents' generosity, gushing from the fount of familial obligation.

'Kak Ngah, Mak and Ayah have something to discuss with you,' her father said one afternoon in their living room. Sitting beside him was her mother, nodding slightly and giving Hafizah the smile of reassurance that Hafizah knew to mean everything was essentially all right, but to expect a serious conversation.

'Mak and I have been talking. We're happy to see you graduate, and now you have a job. That's good, very good. As your parents, we are very happy,' said her father.

As far as family conversations went, Hafizah thought the one they were having would turn out to be about finding her a life partner. Building a mosque together, as the saying goes.

'We see that for young people nowadays, life is very hard. Financially. During Mak and Ayah's time, we could afford a house after working for three to five years. But now, the prices of houses are just too high,' her father declared, the volume shooting up and making him sound like one of those financial gurus who peddle questionable advice on Twitter.

'Okay, Ayah. What you say is right. Why are we talking about houses?'

Her father looked at her mother.

'You tell her.'

'It's nothing, Kak Ngah, just that Ayah and Mak, we worry about our children. What will happen to them when we are gone? We're not rich, but we're blessed, *Alhamdulillah*. So, we want to share our *rezeki* with our children, with you. That's okay right, *sayang*?'

'It's not just okay, Mak, it's very okay. Are you getting me a house?' Hafizah asked cheekily.

'We have some money. It's not a lot. And we want to help you buy property,' her father quipped.

In all honesty, Hafizah would have loved to put any monetary gifts towards travelling instead of a house. But her parents made it clear that any money they would gift could not go to a junket to Machu Picchu or Jeju, for example.

It was a tidy sum, conjured up by cracking the EPF (Employees Provident Fund) egg and cobbling together some savings. Urged by her parents to use it to buy a house, Hafizah resisted, finding everything either not worth the money or aesthetically, rather ghastly.

'I don't know why I should be thrilled when I find a place that is more than a thousand square feet and less than a million ringgit,' she argued. 'This is getting ridiculous, Ayah. I give up,' she told her father after the third weekend in a row looking at show units that seemed to be built by people with the common trait of possessing zero self-awareness. Matchboxes at prices one expects of ritzy penthouses, or condominiums in the eastern ends of the city going for sums that would have one thinking they were sprouting in Bangsar instead of the fringes of Rawang.

'Okay, Kak Ngah. But the best thing to do is to use your money to get more money,' he said, 'and here, if you want to do that, property is the way to go. I've learnt that over the years, and you can see it all around you.'

Hafizah didn't have the heart to tell him that his harping on about appreciating property prices and making money grow more money sounded crass.

She would rather he talked about the All Blacks. Or the weather. Or where in the world his secondary school friends were, and who was a roaring success and who was the sad one who hogged the class WhatsApp group with stories about their not-really-that-great exploits. He could talk about him and Mama during their dating days or the day they first brought Hafizah home from the hospital. Anything but money. Please.

On a drive in Wangsa Maju one afternoon, Hafizah caught sight of a sign, hammered on to a streetlight, saying there were flats up for sale. She knew the ones they were talking about. The formerly white, now closer to the colour of a Siamese cat, five-storey walk-up buildings opposite the school. The ones you could see while you barrel down the slope towards the highway.

Instead of a down payment, why did not she just buy a whole flat? Sure, it would be rinky-dink, and it might be wise to not get too friendly with the neighbours. But she had little need for an infinity pool or a park where one could walk barefoot on pebbles or lounge in a hammock.

'Why would you want to live there? It's not a good area, *lah*, Kak Ngah. What is this?' her father had asked when she declared her intentions. 'I give you some money to help you gain an income in the future and you suggest a flat in Wangsa Maju Section Two?' Never one to show too much emotion, he was perplexed. Not disappointed, just deeply mystified why this particular offspring of his made the choices she did.

'Ayah, I told you from day one that I don't care for a nice house. And I know, you mean to help and I'm always grateful for that. But I don't believe in it, and it stresses me out. People tell me they're now charging rent that's lower than their loan payments, you know? And everyone says there's a bubble. Then you have crappy developers and pushy loan officers who can't answer my questions. Debt! No, when the time comes, I'll move to a kampung house back in Perak. And I don't need lots of property. The other day I heard you and Mama talking, so I know this house is going to be transferred to my name.'

'Hey . . .'

'Which is great thanks, but even if you've changed your mind and now want to give it to Abang or Hezri, that's fine. It'll come back to me someday because I'm going to pull the religion card now and say I know my well-being and upkeep is on them, if I never marry and you're no longer around.'

'I'll make sure you're married before I kick the bucket, young lady. But carry on, I'm listening.'

'So the flat, I want it. Even more than I want a husband,' she said, winking at him. 'Because I want to do something with it. It's *amal jariah*, we can look at it that way.'

'Amal jariah? Are you going to let people live rent-free?'

'No, but I was thinking . . . you know for people in the city, those with young children, life is really tough for them. I was thinking about that and then remembered learning in university about this thing they do in Brazil and Mexico, where the government gives poor families money or some sort of help if they meet certain goals. Like send their kids to school, or make sure they get their injections, eat well. Things like that.'

'Okay, and you want to do something like that with the flat?'

'Yes.'

'But this is Malaysia. Children already go to school and get their injections.'

'Yes, I know that. But I could maybe modify it, like reduce the rent if their kids get good results or have good attendance at school. It'll give the parents an incentive to make sure their kids do well in school. That's something good, right?'

'Yes, it is. But it is also a lot of work. Maybe you think it's a good idea now, but are you sure you want to continue, for ten, twenty years more?'

'Why not? They'd get a place to live, and I'd get to help out. And the money you gave me would be put to good use.'

'But what if people aren't interested? They might think you're being nosy.'

'Well, they aren't the right people for this then. If people want to help, why push them away?'

'Because, sometimes people doubt one's intentions.'

She hoped Zul and his wife did not doubt her intentions. She wasn't hiding anything, and they needed to make space for trust.

But then again, trust is a tricky thing. Hafizah learnt this first-hand from the goings-on in her own family.

The week before, she accompanied her father on a short trip to the kampung.

'Remember, if they serve you any food, you cannot refuse. In the kampung, they feel slighted when you don't try what they serve. Even if you cannot eat a lot, just nibble, okay?' her mother's advice, despite Hafizah having heard the same thing since she was a child, echoed in her mind as she whiled away the time looking out the window of her father's BMW as he sped up the North-South Highway.

Usually, they would spend at least a few nights in the kampung. But because this trip was not one for Raya festivities or extended family cheer at something like a wedding, it was decided that her mother could remain at home.

At the kampung, their relatives were already expecting them.

'Assalamualaikum, Pak Husin. How are you?' Hafizah's father bowed and kissed the hand of his uncle, whom Hafizah addressed as Tok Husin.

'I am well, Alhamdulillah. Where's Rohaya?' the sprightly eighty-plus-year-old asked.

'Oh, she couldn't make it. She had something to do. She sends her salaam.'

'*Waalaikumussalam, warahmatullahi wabarakatuh.*'

Hafizah loved the way things moved a little slower in the kampung. Her father, the seasoned corporate man, became less chatty and eager to share his opinions and more of a silent listener, offering nods and affirmations when the elderly relatives spoke.

After lunch and a tour of Tok Husin's mangosteen and rambutan trees in the garden, they sat in the living room.

Hafizah noticed her father fidget a bit, drumming his fingers on his lap. It was time to broach the chief reason for their trip here.

'Pak Husin, please forgive me, but I came with an intention,' Hafizah's father broke the silence. 'I messaged Ajai already, asking for his help to speak to you. But he said it's better for me to meet you instead. Sorry, ya, Pak Husin.'

Tok Husin nodded quietly.

'The thing is, I got a call from TNB the other day. They asked me to settle the outstanding payment on the electricity bill for this house. I called the district land office and checked, the assessment on this house hasn't been paid in years,' Hafizah noticed a discernible dip in her father's voice.

'I'm sorry to bring this up, Pak Husin, and to burden you, but all these bills, they need to be paid . . .'

Tok Husin couldn't offer any helpful response. At eighty-plus, he shouldn't have to answer questions about money. That is what children are for. But his son, Pak Ajai, was nowhere to be seen. Surely, he knew that they were visiting today. Surely, her father had told him.

In the safer environs of their own home, where they could say what they wanted without worrying that word would travel to unintended ears, Hafizah knew that things here were not okay. Her father owned the house in which Tok Husin lived. It was inherited from his father, Hafizah's grandfather and the son in the family who did well, studying in England and returning to a respectable job in the civil service.

'I know what they say about me; that my father was well off and that we want for nothing. And wonder why I should be so calculating and so stingy with my relatives. But they don't understand. We're not rich. Living in KL isn't like living in the kampung!' expostulated Hafizah's father at dinner one night.

'I've already waived their rent. But now this? Maybe I should make them pay. It might teach Ajai a lesson, that good-for-nothing!'

'Patience, sayang. Don't get stressed out about money and all these matters,' Hafizah's mother said in her singsong, supportive-wife voice.

'This is the problem with our people! They say so much about being respectful, minding your *adab*. How can we have honest conversations if everything needs to be discussed delicately? Your own relatives. They're the worst!'

Hafizah knew that her father was just venting his spleen with all the pent-up frustration. She didn't blame him. After all, annoyance with one's own family members was what roiled the heart the most. You don't know where to put it, that pounding ire when Lazy Cousin doesn't pay his dues and turns a deaf ear to the topic at all gatherings, or when Unpleasant Aunt makes a loud, mocking remark that she considers is humour, but to you it cuts deep.

'Maybe you can show you're serious, *Abah*. Tell Pak Ajai that his family has to move out if he doesn't settle the bills,' suggested Hafizah.

'D'you think this is America, Kak Ngah? You're not over there any more. Here, we don't do that to relatives,' he looked at her wryly.

'Maybe now's a good time to start,' she said, looking down at her plate. She gagged at the bitter shock of a cardamom pod hidden in her rice.

Her phone lit up. It was a message from Zul.

'Cik Hafizah, sorry for being so late. Is your apartment still available?'

The Unknown

The Banyan Tree

Razia Sultana Khan

Neha contemplated the tree. It was colossal. She tried putting her arms around it but covered only half the circumference of the scabrous trunk. The circular strips that coiled around it added to its girth. The tree exuded a susurrus moan and, looking up, Neha saw the leaves ripple although there was no breeze. It felt alive.

Such old trees were held in reverence in most parts of Bangladesh. Sadhus or religious men did *pradakshna* around the tree, circumnavigating it in the morning chanting, 'Salutation to the king of trees!' It was common knowledge that Siddhartha Gautama had chosen a banyan tree to sit under during his days of meditation and gained enlightenment, or bodhi, under the said tree. Into the very fibres of such trees were woven the most fantastic of tales.

All these stories left their indelible mark and if an old tree happened to be in the path of a passer-by, they maintained their distance, observing a reverential silence as quick footsteps took them away from its vicinity.

Neha wouldn't have admitted to believing what she considered 'fanciful tales' associated with old trees. However, her molecular memory that triggered her awareness whenever she came across large trees could not be ignored. Trees were to be venerated; not only were they a big part of Nature—and it was always best to be on good terms with Nature—they were often considered the abode of spiritual creatures, both good and evil, as well as a sanctuary for earthly creatures.

Neha scrutinized the leaves scattered under the tree. It seemed like the fallen leaves had not been disturbed for a long time, a very long time. She moved her right foot in an arch, left to right and back, sweeping the dried and withered leaves that covered the ground. Somewhere at the back of her mind, it occurred to her that these would make excellent kindling for cooking; but obviously, the neighbourhood provided other forms of firewood, if not, why were these still here?

Neha picked up a large heart-shaped leaf with the extended drip tip. Parts of the leaf had disintegrated, leaving behind a tissue of fine veins. The desiccation had made it curl at the edges and it looked like a roll of paper. She fingered the veins, surprised at how soft they felt—almost fuzzy—like a baby's shaved head. The veins clustered together, arranged geometrically, with equal spaces in between. She decided to pick up a few leaves and preserve them between the pages of her diary when she got home.

She picked up one, then another, until she had a whole bunch piled one on top of the other. She looked up and espied Anju, her friend, half-hidden in the tree. She had managed to climb up a couple of branches and was seated with her legs wide apart on a limb.

Anju was using a see-saw motion to cut what looked like a diagonal line into the tree. She had not contended with the resistance she met—the solidity of the wood, withstanding the pressure of her little Swiss Army knife. However, the more the obstruction, the more determined she grew to continue hacking at the tree. She drew back to consider the result of her five minutes of exertion. A somewhat wobbly 'A' stared back at her, the pale internal flesh of the tree contrasting with its dark bark. She had wanted to etch her full name, Anjuman Ara, but after the strenuous effort involved in carving the first letter, decided that 'Anju' would have to do. She turned to Neha who was a couple of feet below her and said, 'Well?'

'Done? Can we go now?'

'You can at least pretend to look,' said Anju in exasperation, 'I've only got the first letter; there are three more letters to go.'

Neha was compelled to look up, squinting in the evening light. The freshly carved bark had resulted in tiny drops of sap seeping out like mini droplets of blood from a fresh cut. In the orange glow, they looked like tears of lava flowing down.

'Perhaps we can come back and finish it later,' Neha murmured.

Anju didn't hear her or, if she did, chose to ignore her and continued with the zigzag motion that made a sound similar to the little insects buzzing about. Neha looked around her once again. The other members of their party were clustered in small groups close to their guest house; some were stretching or flexing their necks, trying to get the stiffness out of their joints, others had moved a little distance away to enjoy the scenery, but no one had ventured as far as the tree.

Anju and Neha were with a group of forty students from a private university on a fifteen-day 'Lived in Field Experience' (LFE) trip. It was part of their course, and although they grumbled and groaned, they had actually looked forward to the trip. Over the years they had heard such varied stories about LFE trips, some exaggerated, some downright fabricated, that all the students secretly looked forward to it although outwardly they never failed to moan and groan and try to find loopholes to get out of going on one.

'Get away from there! Get away from there!' Suddenly, an elderly man with a flaming, henna-dyed beard started shouting at the two girls. He stood at the periphery of the tree, some eight or ten metres away. 'Get down!' he screamed as he caught sight of Anju in the tree.

Neha flinched and instinctively put her hands behind her back, effectively hiding the dry leaves she had picked up.

Anju held her ground, or branch in this case. 'Is this your tree?' There was a glint in her eye.

'What?'

'I asked, does this tree belong to you?' she challenged him.

'Such trees don't "belong" to people, you silly girl,' the man shook his head.

Anju's eyes narrowed; a typical country bumpkin, she concluded. 'It's just a tree. It must belong to someone. Anyway, we're just climbing it, not harming it.' With a flash of bravado, she climbed a little higher.

The man did just the opposite—he took a step backwards.

'Look,' Neha coaxed, forever the mediator, 'It's getting really late.' She turned to the old man conciliatorily, 'We're leaving, Uncle.'

The man's eyes darted to the right and then to the left. He kept tugging at his beard but made no attempt to approach the tree. Anju couldn't read his face. Was it anger or fear? she wondered.

'You'll regret it!' his voice had lost its edge. A weariness, or to be more precise, a sadness had crept into it. He turned and started to walk away, shaking his head.

Anju grinned triumphantly. She had shown him! She was not a 'silly' town girl or a pushover. It struck her that the view would be even better from the top of the tree. She took a step upward and then another. Pleased, she looked around to see if Neha was watching. An anxious pale face was looking up at her.

'Please be careful,' Neha squeaked. Realizing these were not the words she wanted to say, she cajoled, 'Can we go now? The old man might come back and it'll be dark soon.' After a pause she added, 'We were told to gather in the dining hall after evening prayers.'

'Plenty of time. You go if you want to.' Anju looked at the west horizon where a very bright orange sun was playing havoc with the sky. She didn't really enjoy climbing trees and had only ventured to climb this one to defy Neha. But enough was enough, and she could feel a chill in the air. It should have been pleasant after the warm day, but it was not.

Neha frowned. It was already late. She didn't want to deal with any of the faculty on her own.

In no rush, Anju made the motion of wiping her knife on the tree and said, 'Look! You've got to agree that's neat!' Receiving no reply, she started her descent.

Suddenly the lateness of the hour hit her and without waiting for Neha, she made as if to move towards the compound, but stopped midway.

'What now?' spluttered Neha.

'Can't you feel it?'

'What?'

'Something in the air . . .' Anju wrapped her arms around herself, rubbing her forearms where goosebumps had formed.

'It's called oxygen,' Neha gave an uneasy giggle. 'It's something we're not used to in Dhaka. With the sun gone down, the temperature has fallen.'

'Yeah, that must be it.'

They hurried into the compound and there, right in front of them, was Mr Aslam, the faculty-in-charge.

'What have you young ladies been up to? You do know we're meeting in the dining hall in half an hour.'

'No one told us! Neha, did you know?' Anju turned to Neha and gave her a half-wink.

'Hurry up, hurry up!' Mr Aslam said in a distracted voice, his attention drawn to a couple who had emerged from behind a building.

Before entering their building, Anju turned around to get another glimpse of the tree. It was majestic. From a distance, in the semi-dark, it looked like a giant mushroom or a nuclear explosion.

Mr Aslam announced his arrival with a few resounding claps, 'All boys in building A, all girls take the other building. You can take any room you want as long as there are two to a room.'

There was a rush into the boys' building as they tried to commandeer the better rooms. The girls headed towards the other building, just as quickly but with an outward show of nonchalance. Riffat Begum, in charge of the female students in building B, quickly got to work ushering them to their respective rooms. She had checked out the rooms on the floor for herself and decided that the corner room was the best. Not only did it have a majestic view of the village, with a banyan tree in the background, there was only one bed in it. There was no danger of having to share the room with any of the junior faculty.

They assembled in the dining room for dinner at 8.30 p.m., and then were given one hour of free time. They broke into little groups, one going off to enjoy a puff in the privacy of the back of the building while a few gathered around the custodian to find out if he knew anything about the history of the place.

The custodian was a short, elderly man with a kindly face. 'You're the first group to come here in a long time,' he said.

'Oh really? Why is that? This place seems ideal for large groups,' said someone.

'The owners don't seem to favour letting it out to young people.'

'Why should they care as long as they make money?'

The custodian kept his peace.

Anju had been pondering over the outburst of the elderly man with the henna-dyed beard. She was not used to being chastised, not least by some stranger with a flaming beard. She resented that they had been caught off their guard at the banyan tree. If we had been in Dhaka, I would've shown him some, she thought fuming to herself. And here was another old geezer making disparaging remarks against young people.

'What do you have against young people?' Anju remarked truculently.

'It's not all young people. Well, some, you have to admit, are quite arrogant . . .'

'Come on! We could say the same about old . . . I mean elderly people,' piped up another voice.

'Please, hear me out. Some young people have no respect for . . . older people, Nature . . .'

'Hold it there, Uncle. I beg to differ. I think it's our generation who do more to conserve nature: recycle, conserve energy, plant trees.'

'Yeah, your generation did its part in messing it all up,' added another male voice.

'I didn't mean it that way. I agree that some young people are very aware of what we owe Nature. I meant . . .' he made to get up from the rocking chair in which he had ensconced himself and said in a cheerful voice, 'It's getting late. Plenty of time to talk tomorrow.'

'We're not letting you off that easy, Uncle. You started it. Might as well continue. Come, tell us what we're doing wrong. Do tell.'

The man allowed his body to sag into the curve of the chair, then said in a tired voice, 'You lack belief.'

'Oh, come now. What has religion got to do with this? My belief is my belief. How does that affect ecology?'

'You're not getting my point.'

'Well, tell us so we get your point.'

'You think you know everything. You have a scientific reason for everything you see. But there are things that science cannot explain.' There was a pause, but no one felt inclined to interrupt. 'You see a beautiful river flowing its course and you know that the water started as a spring up in some mountain. There is rain and you know how that happens. A beautiful tree, and you'll be able to name the different parts and the purpose and the—'

'Anything wrong with that?' Anju butted in.

'No, but there's another side, another dimension. Our elders had beliefs and we need to respect that.'

Anju yawned widely, making no attempt to hide it. Obviously, someone who liked to hear the sound of his voice;

and now he had an audience. She closed her eyes letting the voices flow around her.

'Take that banyan tree for example.'

Both Anju's and Neha's ears perked up.

They all turned to look out of the window, but the panes mirrored only the darkness. 'Well, what do you see?'

'A banyan tree,' Anju tittered.

A few other students joined in with a snigger or two.

'Yes, a banyan tree but it isn't just any old tree.' The custodian stopped. His eyes closed as if he were mining through his memory chest. His face reflected displeasure. For a couple of minutes, the only sound was the squeak of his rocking chair as he rocked to and fro, to and fro.

'Ehm, ehm!' one of the students cleared his throat.

The custodian opened his eyes. They were blank. The students tittered. Had the old geezer dozed off—right in the middle of his own story?

'Yes?' Neha prompted him.

'There's a story surrounding that tree. A long time ago, a very long time ago, when all around was the jungle and that tree, a sapling among many others, a young girl, hardly a woman, was brought here and married off to the tree.' The old man stopped and sighed. He had managed to snag their interest.

'You think this is all fiction, but such things did happen. If a young girl was widowed, her parents, to save her from the walls of the ashram, a lifestyle which deprived the girl of most pleasures of life, would take her to the interior of the jungle and marry her to a tree. It then became her duty to look after the tree and make sure it survived and flourished. As long as the tree survived, she was considered a married woman.

'But that's barbaric!' expostulated a squeaky voice.

'How could the girl survive by herself?' someone demanded.

'The forest, and a tree for that matter, is a good provider— if you survive. You get shade, protection . . . and when people come to offer their prayers, food.'

'People? In the middle of the jungle?'

The custodian continued in a soft monotone, 'In the beginning, the girl thought someone would rescue her and bided her time. As days passed and then months, and no one came, a resentment started to fester within her. She remembered how happy she'd been, playing with her brothers and sisters. Why should she be made to live alone, away from everyone, because her husband had died? A husband she didn't know and had only seen, or rather felt during the wedding—like a shadow beside her? She roamed around listlessly, forgetting to pray to the tree or water it. One evening, as she sat at its trunk etching lines on the soft earth with a long knife her father had left with her for her protection, she started making playful jabs at the elevated trunk. At some point, the mindless play turned aggressive as all her accumulated frustration and resentment converged.

'The leaves of the tree made swishing noises although there was no breeze and she felt a shudder go through it.

'A holy man who was passing by some distance away heard a shrill scream. Upon drawing near, he saw a young woman lying under a banyan tree with long scratches all over her body. There was no one in sight, so he carried her to the nearest village to see if anyone could help her. The marks soon vanished but her eyes remained blank. It is said that travellers sometimes see an old woman roaming the woods.'

'So?'

'What happened to her?'

'Did she recover?'

'Who knows,' the custodian shrugged. 'During the full moon, wails can be heard from the forest.'

'It's a forest, of course there are wild animals. It could be a wolf or a jackal.'

'Believe what you will. Notice, though, this is the only banyan tree around here. The other trees were cut down as people moved in. But no one wants to touch that tree.'

There was a moment of silence with each person lost in his or her own thoughts. Suddenly a momentary breeze drew in a soft wail from the distance, the sound increasing slowly, then subsiding in a moan. The students looked at each other but said nothing. The custodian's jaw clenched but he kept his eyes glued to the floor.

'Scary!' Anju stretched the vowel for full effect and then, giving a shaky laugh, got up. 'On that note, I think I'll be off to bed.'

After dinner, Riffat Begum, the faculty member, went up to her room. When she had come earlier, she had been pleasantly surprised at how bright and well-lit it was. A smallish room with a wooden, four-poster bed in the middle. There was a desk with an empty flower vase, and a large floor-length mirror beside it. Two large windows looked out into the adjoining field. The banyan tree occupied most of the frame, and Riffat's heart contracted at how elegant and graceful it looked. She found herself reaching out to it. It seemed so close that one could almost touch it. Pity she had left her water colours at home.

She stood at the window, contemplating the tree. It was truly magnificent. Even in the darkness, it seemed to wield power. With a sigh, she closed the window and drew the curtains. There were probably swarms of mosquitoes out there and in all likelihood, they had already invaded the room. She was glad she was by herself. She had a full hour to do some writing.

With a happy heart, she opened her red, leather diary and started journaling the events of her day.

Something was pushing Riffat down, the grip strong around her neck. She gasped for breath and with great effort, pushed off the weight. Her eyes opened. She was still at her desk with the diary open in front of her and the mother of all pains at the base of her neck. How long had she been sleeping? She flexed her shoulders, then interlocked her fingers and lifted them together over her head to activate her muscles. She got up to go to the restroom. On the way, she paused at the mirror beside the desk.

At first, she couldn't make out what it was. Then, she saw the trunk and the branches of the banyan tree. She whipped around and looked at the window. The yellow curtains regarded her silently. Forehead furrowed, she felt her body break into sweat. She turned back to the mirror. *How?* As Riffat moved closer to the mirror and entwined in the reflection of the tree, she saw her own. But her face? That distorted image? The red-hot eyes, the twisted lips with a silent scream snaking out of it?

Riffat stood motionless. She could hear the pounding of her heart—in her neck, her throat, her ears—but she couldn't move; she was rooted to the spot.

Another scream, this time from outside, merged with the one from her reflection and she extricated herself from the reflection and stumbled out of the room.

There was pandemonium outside as the scream followed her and seemed to be echoing from all directions. The entrance to the last room in that corridor was blocked by a number of students. Riffat Begum pushed her way in.

Anju was lying on the narrow bed. Her shalwar had been pulled down and the kameez pulled up slightly exposing her legs. Riffat's initial reaction was to shout, 'All boys out!' but her eyes were drawn to Anju's legs. The flesh of her legs was exposed as if someone had slashed parallel lines with a razor. There was no blood, just raw, pink flesh. After a stunned moment, Riffat Begum shouted, 'All boys out!'

The next time she looked around, the bed was encircled by wide-eyed girls.

Anju lay spreadeagled on the bed like a starfish. She didn't move but every so often, a tremor pulsed through her. Her face was as white as a sheet. Her eyes were open but only the whites showed.

'Anju! Anju! Are you okay?' Even as she said the words, Riffat realized how trite they sounded. She turned to the other girls, 'What happened?'

'She was fine until a few minutes ago.'

'She said she didn't feel too well,' another added.

'The bed started shaking!'

'That's because she lay down.'

'I thought it was an earthquake!'

'Stop!' Riffat held up her hands to stop the incoherent words. 'Who was actually here? Okay, Neha, you tell me. Slowly.'

'We had dinner, then came up,' Neha mumbled. She stopped and looked across at the window. The window was closed and the curtain drawn.

'Then?' Riffat prodded.

'I ... ah ... went to the ... you know ... the restroom.' She stopped again, glancing towards the door. She folded her arms and moved closer to the girl next to her.

'I ... ehm ... told her to close the window. Mosquitoes.' She stopped again, running her tongue over her lips and gulping a couple of times. 'When I returned, she was lying on the bed,' she made the motion of scratching her own arms, 'scratching . . . like crazy.'

'She was also making weird noises,' another girl interjected.

'She kept saying, "Get away, get away!"' Neha whispered.

'Those marks . . .' Riffat Begum tried to control her voice but a quaver escaped.

'She kept scratching herself,' Neha continued. 'I thought, perhaps some insect . . . you know . . . had gotten into her clothes.' She paused again. Her eyes wandered around the room, 'I . . . asked her to take them off. We helped to untie her shalwar and pull it down. That's when we noticed those marks.' Riffat had to strain to hear the last few words.

'You mean she made those?' Riffat looked at the long parallel lines.

'Do they look self-inflicted?' another girl piped up.

'What else could it be? Turn her around,' Riffat said to Anju. Two of the girls turned her over. Riffat pulled up the kameez. The same flayed flesh met their eyes.

No one voiced the obvious question.

'Turn her back and cover her with something.'

As the girls went to find another sheet, Riffat Begum peered at the marks on Anju's legs. Even as she watched, the red blotches seemed to subside, and the flesh retreated inside. After a couple of minutes, the legs were back to normal.

'What did you do?' Neha exploded, full of admiration.

'Nothing. Absolutely nothing.'

'But . . . but . . .'

It was another twenty minutes before Anju was conscious of her surroundings.

'What happened?' she moaned.

'You tell us!'

'I had a weird dream,' Anju's voice sounded as if it were coming from afar. 'The banyan tree . . . it came into the room and . . . and . . . climbed all over me.' She closed her eyes and her body started trembling.

'Are you okay now?' Neha asked.

'Of course, I'm okay,' Anju whispered. She turned to Neha with sightless eyes.

The Ruined Hotel

Danton Remoto

'Ma'am, please don't forget to ask them for the winning lotto numbers,' Mang Senyong, the school-bus driver, reminded me with his trademark smirk as I alighted from the bus. And then, he grinned widely, his front teeth yellowed with nicotine.

But before I could answer, Lito, a member of the academic staff, had already answered for all of us. 'Of course,' he said. 'Then, we can all share the prize of 250 million pesos for the mega lotto!' The rest of the people in the bus—mostly academic staff having a writing workshop in Baguio, and I, the visiting journalist—snickered. Of course, I thought, a lotto windfall would be welcomed. Times had been bad—with the Philippine peso pegged at 60 pesos to the US dollar, rice selling at 50 pesos a kilo and every other Filipino wanting to work abroad as a caregiver. A deep state of depression had begun to grip the country. The taste of ashes was on everyone's tongue.

I checked the time on my big, round watch: 10 p.m. The frigid mountain air chilled me the moment I got off the school bus. Why, I thought, it's even colder out here in the open air than inside that air-conditioned bus! It was 7 December and frost was forecast in the towns north of Baguio. Etta, the head of university publications, a tall, talkative woman who had been my classmate in high school, had asked me to train her staff.

So, I took a week's break from teaching English as a second language to Vietnamese refugees in Morong, Bataan. I took the five-hour bus ride to Quezon City, slept over at Etta's house, and now here I was in Baguio, where the fog was rolling down the sad, green hills.

It was also a visit I was hesitant to make. I had just broken up with Jey (short for Jeyaretnam), my Indian boyfriend, a year ago. I met him in one of those Asian conferences where teachers update one another on twenty-first-century pedagogy and the Asian ways. I was standing near the coffee stand when this tall, good-looking gentleman said, 'Excuse me', and reached for the milk for his cup of tea.

Being a cheerful and hospitable Filipino, I smiled at him, and he smiled back, and we began to talk. He was a graduate of the University College in London where he had completed an undergraduate programme in international relations with journalism and political science. He won me over with his elegant accent and deep baritone, as well as his keen mimicry of the favourite words spoken by the Filipinos in London. Our new heroes, the *Bagong Bayani*, our overseas Filipino workers—the entertainers, house maids and IT personnel— taught their foreigner friends a gaggle of words ranging from *kumusta ka na?* to *putang ina mo!* I told him to remember the first phrase since it was a warm and sincere greeting, often prefaced with 'have you eaten?' and just drop the second phrase, which cast aspersions on one's beloved mother.

Jey also looked like a Bollywood movie star. He was tall, lean and muscular, and he was the most courteous man I had ever met. He always punctuated his words with 'I'm sorry', his eyes deep and penetrating, his moustache and beard black as night. He was always asking me what I wanted the week he visited the Philippines, whether we were at a fine-dining restaurant in Trinoma or at the bustling mall in Ortigas or lining up at the cinema houses in Gateway. Unlike Filipino men, who were spoiled rotten by their mothers, Jey worked his way to his postgraduate studies and did all the household chores, from cooking the best biryani to pressing long-sleeved shirts without leaving a wrinkle even at the collar.

In short, he would have been the perfect boyfriend—and the perfect butler. I loved him with passion, even if my crazy Filipino friends sometimes teased me for being 'The Curry Queen'.

He visited the Philippines in December last year. We were in Manila for three days, and then we went to Baguio because he found the noxious air of Manila bad for his asthma. We avoided Session Road since it was also crowded with tourists and was choked with diesel fumes. We stayed in a cosy and quiet hotel in the suburbs.

He laughed mightily, his voice rolling inside the small store in the public market. When I pulled down the wooden barrel, the wooden figure's dick sprang to life for all the world to see. He looked away from the young boys in loincloth catching a rain of coins being thrown by the tourists in the promontory of Mines View Park.

Jars of purple yam and strawberry jam filled our white recycled bags as we left the Good Shepherd Convent. We strolled in Burnham Park and on the wide pedestrian walkways, the sky a brilliant canvas of blue, marvelling at the sunflowers following the path of the sun. And in the hotel room, after the conversation and the hugs and the warm words whispered into each other's ears, we made love. Outside, in December's deep night, the windows began to be covered with mist.

* * *

But this December, a year later, I was again in Baguio City because of Etta. She was the kind of friend who would listen to you at 4 a.m. I could not turn down her request to help their academic staff. At the end of our dinner a fortnight ago, while sipping her favourite cappuccino, she even told me, 'Well, it's been a year since you and your Indian gentleman went to Baguio. I think it's time that you return and bury the bones of that beast!' I laughed my usual laughter—a cackle really, like a hen about to lay a big, fat egg—although a black and invisible veil suddenly fell over my face.

But today, I was going down the school bus with Etta and her staff to watch the Spirit Warriors at the Baguio Terraces Hotel. This was the favourite hotel of the dictator and his wife. The staff wanted to see the Spirit Warriors appease the spirits that allegedly still roamed the hotel that was flattened by a strong earthquake ten years ago—or what used to be the hotel. For now, in front of me, was just a wall of galvanized iron sheets painted green enclosing the area where the hotel used to be. The grand entrance was no longer there. That was where the limousine of the dictator and his extravagant wife would stop. He would then alight, the gold medals from the battles he had won shining on his military uniform. She would follow suit, dripping with diamonds and on her neck, a lace of rubies the colour of blood.

Lito knocked, and a guard in white-and-blue uniform opened the gate. Lito spoke to him and the guard opened the gate.

The ruins of the hotel where almost 500 people died had been cleared. Not a stone remained standing. And the Spirit Warriors were already there—a group of teenagers together with Merlin, their mentor. Merlin was also a writer of amazing fiction and a friend of mine. He walked over to us and told me, 'Hey, Rose, you cannot just watch the Spirit Warriors. We want the observers to be participants as well. So, you and the lady alongside, you should go there!' Merlin pointed towards a place in the distance that was pitch black.

Melody, the secretary of the department of English, held my hand. Reluctantly, I followed her and the ten teenagers in the direction where Merlin said we should go.

It was on a spot parallel to the north end of the street. I had been stupid enough not to bring my cardigan, and so, in my plain T-shirt, I felt cold as I walked. When I looked up, the stars seemed to shiver in the dark sky as well.

'Let us form a circle in this area,' said Ding-Dong, our leader, hitting the ground with the end of his cane hewn out of rough wood. We followed his instructions. And then, he began to chant, 'God of Light, please bless us in this undertaking to bring peace to the souls of the disturbed.' He chanted the phrase three times. The silence was thick. Suddenly, he stopped. 'Someone is here.'

I looked to my left, then to my right. But there was nobody.

Ding-Dong continued in a more formal tone to address someone whom I could not see. 'Good evening. We are here at the Baguio Terraces Hotel because we have been asked to help the spirits still roaming in this place. We have been asked to liberate them from this prison house of memories.'

Silence.

Ding-Dong explained to us in a softer, conspiratorial voice, 'It is a man and he asked me who I am, so I told him about us and our undertaking.' Then he continued speaking to the darkness beyond. 'There was a major earthquake here ten years ago, with an intensity of 7.5 The hotel was completely destroyed. I'm sorry—I'm sorry, but you were one of those who died.'

Silence.

The pitch of Ding-Dong's voice began to rise. He seemed agitated. 'He is angry with us. He says I am lying! Quick, let us share with him our own pain to make him understand that he is not alone in his suffering. We have to empathize with him. Okay, you share with us first,' he added, pointing at the girl who sat across from me.

'Okay,' the girl said. 'Good evening,' and then continued in a Los Angeles Valley accent, 'I wanna share with you my pain, mister. Coz, you know, one time, I went home really super late and I wuz kinda drunk so my dad and mom had me grounded, you know. They didn't allow me to drive my car for a week.' Then the pitch of her voice began to rise. 'It was so painful coz I had to take public transport for one week. It was hell for me!'

I looked at Barbie and wished the ground beneath her feet would just crack open and swallow her up.

'Is there anybody else who wants to share his or her pain?' Ding-Dong asked. 'Quick, guys, because he's starting to get really angry. In fact, he is now shooing us away!'

'Well,' began the boy to the left of Barbie. He was fair-skinned, with long and layered hair like a young Korean pop singer. He was wearing a new denim jacket in full-blooded blue. 'I failed calculus last semester and so my parents, you know how strict they are, right? They didn't take me with them when they went to the Maldives. I had to take up calculus again during summer classes and had to be contented with swimming in our pool at home.'

Maybe piranhas ought to have been let loose in that pool, I thought. I gave him a cold look.

Suddenly, my thighs and legs felt like they were being punctured by many pins and needles. The tingling pain crept swiftly over my whole body, followed by a heaviness that fell on my nape, my shoulders and then my back. It felt like a big boulder had been placed on my back. Then I felt my head start to swell.

I began to see him, amorphous at first, like wavy lines of smoke, then slowly corporealizing into something solid and visible. He was in a white, long-sleeved shirt. His blue jeans were faded. He was seated on a brown sofa with soft cushions. His head rested on his left arm. He seemed to be asleep. There was a sudden and powerful jolt, which made his sofa dart violently to the right. He woke up with a start. Panic-stricken people ran around him, past him. Screams rent the air. He saw them as if in a blur. Only the voices were there—a splinter of voices in his ears. When he looked up, the ceiling was cracking, and then the concrete floor imploded beneath him and the ceiling crumbled down upon him along with the reinforcing iron rods.

But he thinks it was just a dream. He was waiting for Jeremy to come back to the hotel from the Good Shepherd Convent. Jeremy liked purple yam and strawberry jams, and their stock had run out. He was waiting for Jeremy because, when he came back, they would go for a walk. They would stroll down the wide sidewalk in Burnham Park in the cool, bracing air, and admire the sunflowers planted on terraces cut into the hills.

I did speak to him. I didn't know why I should do so, but I did. When I spoke to him, my voice seemed to come from a source inside me, a source deeper than my blood. I told him that he was not dreaming and that he must let go. A strong earthquake rippled through the whole island of Luzon. The hotel crumbled. None of the hotel guests survived the sudden crash of thick concrete and twisted iron bars. All that happened ten long years ago.

Then I told him; I didn't know why, but I told him in a voice like black and bitter water, that my boyfriend, Jey, would never return to me as well—that he had been diagnosed with leukaemia. All his blood had to be drained and a fresh infusion of plasma had to be pumped back into his body. This had to be done every six months. The cocktail of drugs and steroids had bloated his body. The pain must have been unbearable, but he never told me about it. He just sent a text message at the crack of dawn, a year ago. When I woke up, there was a text message in my mobile phone and I read it with my eyes still heavy with sleep.

I have an e-mail for you, the message read. I thought I was just being tugged away from the depths of a dream.

I turned off my mobile phone and turned it on again. I was sure that the message would be gone when I turned on my mobile phone. But the words were still there: white, icy letters in the black void. In the half-light cast by my bedside lamp, I fumbled for my laptop and turned it on. I read his email. The words were scissors that cut my intestines into shreds. Leukaemia. Cannot be with you any more. Don't want you to take care of me. Have to go. Do not call. Do not text. Do not write to me any more. Have a great life. Good luck.

Good luck. He had said it like he was a guest speaker at a graduation ceremony; telling a thousand, fresh-faced young people, 'Well, all of you guys, have a great life and good luck: I hope all of your dreams will come true.'

In the days that followed, I felt like the tiny, white dot on our old television set, the dot getting smaller and smaller until it finally vanished into the black screen. But I still reported for work in the office, hoping the workload would deaden me. My English as second language students must have wondered why I would seem to float into space when our English lessons touched on the words 'distance' and 'alone'. When my eyes would blur, I would walk calmly to the bathroom, shut the door and weep.

But the world did not crumble. The days slipped into weeks, stretched into months and a year went by. There was a vacant room inside myself but it had slowly begun to shrink . . .

* * *

Suddenly, I shivered. My hand clutched my chest. It was painful, as if a strong fist had gripped my heart and was wringing it, again and again. My shirt became wet with the tears I didn't know I was shedding. In the chaos, I heard Melody talking. 'Ma'am? Ma'am? Are you all right, ma'am?'

Just then, I felt a bolt of red-light streak from my heart. It zigzagged down to my intestines, down to my groin and thighs, down to my legs and feet, then it went up again. Its movement was swift and painful. In a flash, the red light blazed past my head. Like a torch of fire, it erupted and shot up into the cold and black sky.

'He has left,' Ding-Dong said just in time, 'he has moved on to the next world.'

Melody was hugging me. She was wiping my face with her handkerchief. She repeatedly asked, 'What happened, ma'am? Are you okay, ma'am?'

My eyes opened. I felt so tired, as if I had just come from a very faraway place. I took her handkerchief and wiped the tears from my face. I looked at her. I spoke haltingly. 'Nothing, Melody. I . . . nothing . . . happened to me.'

Melody just nodded and tried to smile. The teenagers also asked me if I was all right.

'I'm fine,' I said, 'thank you.' I checked the time on my big, round watch. It was almost one in the morning.

* * *

Back at the hotel, I sat in the twenty-four-hour restaurant and ordered a cup of decaffeinated Earl Grey tea. I knew that this was not the way to drink tea, as somebody I used to love would often tell me, 'this tea is defanged of its bergamot and its bite.' But I also wanted to calm down and have a good sleep afterward. After finishing the cup of tea, I walked to the lift and went to my room on the fourth floor. I took a warm shower, letting the healing water and the green, olive-oil soap cleanse me of everything that had stained me. I changed into my pyjamas. I shut the windows, pulled the drapes and locked the door. Then, I turned off all the lights. But I took a peek outside the window, into the solid darkness. I saw the trees. The trees had leaves like fingers. Somebody is waving at me, I thought. But later, I decided it was just the whorl of leaves awakened by a passing breeze.

And sleep I did after a few minutes—the kind of sleep I had not had in a year. It was a sleep, long and peaceful—a sleep hardly troubled by dreams.

One Night in Cao Zhou

Samuel P. Boucher / William Quill

The evening sun shone brightly over the low, rolling hills. The hills were green with patches of bright flowers, spread along the main road from Kiautschou. A woman in flowing, blue robes slowed her large, white horse. We've come a long way, but we're finally here, thought the young woman sadly. The horse trotted in an almost meandering way in the brisk autumn evening. The woman's hair was gathered into several knots and yet, it still flowed in the direction of the wind. She lifted her hand to block out the blinding twilight and squinted. In the distance, between the hills, was a familiar sight. It was a small town with flat-roofed buildings laid out in a linear pattern along the dirt road. It was the town of Cao Zhou, sometimes called 'Mudan'. It was the woman's home.

If the woman kept going down the long road, she would come to the Yellow River and the Henan province. The Henan province, where the Middle Kingdom began and Confucian civilization flourished. Back the way she came, past the Anji River with its overpriced ferry, there was the road to Kiautschou. Kiautschou was the province that the Qing had leased to the Germans out of their port of Tsingtao. Cao Zhou was in southwestern Kiautschou; it was the furthest city in the province under the Kaiser's sphere of influence. Thus, it was largely outside of his control.

The girl remembered the city fondly despite her many years away being educated in Shanghai. It was the quaint and sleepy little town of her youth known for its cultivation of flowers. She remembered the warmth of the summertime. She remembered how the rolling fields would be alive with flowers of pink and violet in the rainless spring. It was autumn now and it was cool and brisk dry air but without the cold of the winter months to come.

The woman looked out into the hexagonal fields of peony, watching the farmers tend to their flowers. As the woman daydreamed of times gone by, she found herself within the confines of the town. Her horse strutted up to the main market in town.

At the doorway of the grocer, a little girl in a brown dress stood sweeping the dust out from in front of the shop. Her expression brightened when she looked up and saw the woman in blue approaching.

'Hua Feng? Hua Feng, is it really you? It is! It is!' the young girl squealed as she threw down her broom and ran into Hua Feng's open arms.

'Hello, sweet Li Ji,' said Hua Feng. 'Yes, I have returned . . . how is your granny?'

'Not old enough to be deaf. I could have heard Ji's screams from a mile away.' Appearing in the threshold of the door was an old, old woman. Her face carried the weight of a thousand lifetimes, but her eyes were as sharp as an owl in the nighttime sky.

She spat on the dirt in front of Hua Feng. 'So, you've returned from the big city, have you? Gotten a whole headful of that foreign education? You missed the funeral, you know. It was yesterday while you were meandering your way here on that big bulox.'

Hua Feng slid down her stallion with a plop on the dirt road. Uncaring of her beautiful patterned blue dress, Hua bent down and prostrated herself before Granny Li. 'I came as soon as I heard. While my pace was fast initially, when I realized that I would not make it in time for the funeral according to Han burial rites, I decided to ease up on poor Mai Bai here. I humbly beg you for your forgiveness, Madam Li.'

Granny Li stroked her many wrinkles downward. 'Well, well,' said Granny Li modestly, although her eyes shone approval. 'No need to be so traditional about it all. Here now, get off that dirty ground and come in and have some tea.'

* * *

Hua Feng felt herself pulled inside the shop by little Li Ji excitedly. Inside the shop with its white walls and green pillars, Hua Feng was hit by a wall of aroma. She smelled baked bread, bringing back a flood of memories and emotions. She saw herself as a young girl running in between tables and chairs and wares, chasing a young boy screaming from fright. Her eyes welled up, and her voice cracked when she asked, 'Where did it happen?'

'There,' pointed Granny Li with a nod.

Hua Feng looked across the store to the wooden floor near the entrance to the cellar. The wood was blotched with a disturbingly red stain. Without a word, Hua Feng faced forward and followed Granny Li upstairs to the small living quarters above the shop.

Sitting on her knees around a short table, Hua Feng raised a small cup that Granny Li had handed her and took a deep breath. She smelled the floral aroma of the peony-infused green tea with a slight hint of the incense burning in the corner altar, where the ancestral paintings were hung.

Nearly everything in Cao Zhou had signs of peony. These delicate pink flowers were the national flower of the Qing, and the whole community was bent towards its cultivation. It was infused into every aspect of their life. Patterned on their clothes. Ingested medicinally. Put in their food. And yes, even infused in their green tea. Peony was the lifeblood of Cao Zhou. It was Hua Feng's lifeblood.

'I am afraid that this is all my fault,' sobbed Hua Feng. 'I have a feeling that this is because I am a Manchu that this happened to Li Yen. All of these Han bands are stirring up hatred against the Qing—and against the Manchu people. It is not MY fault I was born a Manchu instead of a Han.'

'There, there, dear. It will all be all right. I am sure there are some fools who may give you bitter looks, but I can assure you that no one—no, not a single person in this family, blames you,' Granny Li stated, lightly patting Hua on her back.

Hua Feng wiped her eyes and composed herself as befitting a Manchu.

'Thank you, Madam Li.'

* * *

'Junjun!' came a sudden cry. The ladies looked up to see old man Wen looking at Hua Feng with a startled look. 'It . . . it is you . . . you're back. I thought I saw you trot-trot-trotting your way into town. Eh, uh . . . how wonderful!'

'Thank you, Wen. You don't have to call me that any more, though. It seems like those days are over. The Republicans are

advancing on the capital, and they mean to depose Emperor
Puyi. And with the end of him, the end of noble titles.'

'Oh no!' growled old man Wen defiantly. 'I will never stop
calling you Junjun! That is the way of the world. We need
nobility like we need parents. It is the whole order of things!
How are we going to go on without the order of things!'

'Calm yourself. We will go on as we always have.'

'No, oh no, no, no! There is a way of things. Way things
should be. There are peasants and they produce peasants, and
then there are nobles who marry nobles to prod—' old man
Wen stopped abruptly at his gaffe. 'Uh, princess, that's not, uh
what I mean is . . .'

'It's all right, Wen. No harm was meant. Now, if you
would please see yourself out. I have some things I would like
to discuss with Granny Li.'

'Ah, yes . . . of course,' mumbled Wen as he fumbled down
the stairs and out of the shop.

Granny Li eyes Hua Feng intently. 'Oh, yes? What are
those things you wish to discuss with me?'

'Li Yen. Li Yen and his father's death. Your son and your
grandson's death. MY husband-to-be's death.'

'And what of it?'

'I am going to bring them to justice.'

Granny Li chortled, 'And how is that?

'Do not forget who I am. We, Manchus, are not ones to
trifle over such things. I will find his murderers and bring
them to justice—with or without your help.'

'I admire your ferocity, Hua,' said Granny Li quietly.
'I think I felt the same way when my husband died during the
Taiping Rebellion. But these things are better left alone. Trust
me. Digging into them will only bring pain and guilt. You are
young, child. I beg you. Go on living. Just live.'

Hua Feng stood up suddenly and stormed out of the room. Granny Li and Li Jen called after her, running down the stairs. Hua stopped at the threshold. She glanced at the two women, both survivors in their own way, and she felt a terrible wave of guilt wash over her. She ran back to them and hugged them in a fierce embrace. 'I'm sorry, Madam Li, but this is what I have to do.'

'Then go in peace, child,' said Granny Li quietly, cupping Hua's face in her hands.

* * *

Hua bowed one final time to Granny Li and waved to little Ji. The sun had set; however, Hua knew she could find her way. She continued on down the road to her next stop: the local police precinct. The shutters of the small town rattled as the wind swept through the long street. Almost as if the town itself was trembling. It gave Hua Feng an unfriendly feeling. Maybe this is not the town I grew up in after all, she thought. She turned the corner and made her way to the small building at the end of the side street. She took a deep breath and pushed open the door, entering the police station. In the office, there was a single desk with a single pot of water, a single cup of water, a single plate of boiled peony roots and a single writing quill. Sitting at the desk, there was a young, narrow-faced man with black hair. His hair was long but done up in a messy topknot with strands of hair falling in every direction over his head. Hua gasped.

'Hello, can I help you—Hua! Is that you?'

Hua Feng took a step back startled. 'Chen?'

'What are you doing here?' they both responded in unison. 'I'm the new police deputy, Hua,' Chen laughed nervously.

'What happened to Ta Bai?'

Chen looked down for a moment and looked up into Hua's eyes.

'Listen, Hua. I think you should take a seat. Would you like some water?'

'No, I just had tea with Granny Li.'

'Right,' said Chen as he poured himself a cup of water. 'Well . . . things are different in the interior than in the coast, Hua. The gunboats of the Europeans keep the bandits at bay there, but here, we get attacked. It used to be rare. Just once or twice a year. But things are changing fast since the death of the dowager empress. Now, we get attacked almost once a month. Sometimes it's the Republican troops; sometimes it's the emperor's troops. This past year, it was a new group. Some anti-Manchu group, who call themselves the Gelaohui. They are calling for all Hans to unite and kick the Manchus back to the north. They are attacking every village and murdering the Christian missionaries—including the ones who set up the hospital. Anyways, Mudan doesn't do much business, so there isn't much to take—so . . . so they take what they can. When Ta Bai tried to put a stop to their games . . . he disappeared.'

'I'm sorry, Chen.'

'We have only been able to stave them off due to the Dadao Hui.'

'The Da-what?'

'They are a group that are a part of the Big Sword Society. They guard small villages and towns from the roving bandits for a fee.'

'How much?'

'Why is that importan—?'

'I was the Junjun of this prefecture at one time, Chen. I want to know how much?'

Chen quieted for a few moments, and then said, 'Half.'

'Half? Half of what?'

'Half of the profit from the royal peonies sales.'

Hua was shocked. That was most of the money the village would need to purchase supplies for winter.

'Chen, how could you let this happen? This is extortion, Chen!'

'Don't you think we knew that?' snapped Chen bitterly. 'We had no choice. It was that or we would be ruined by the bandits. At least, we can deal with these bandits peacefully.'

Hua shook her head in disbelief. These Dadao Hui— whoever they were—were enriching themselves by levying their own taxes among the poor peasants. She looked again at the peony roots on the table.

'I've been chewing on them. They're for my headaches,' answered Chen without looking at the roots.

'I see,' Hua sighed. 'I don't know what to say . . . I never realized it had gotten so bad in the interior.'

'Yeah . . . well, we have to keep going, I guess,' replied Chen solemnly, then attempting to change the topic asked, 'Anyways, I heard you were off in Shanghai at some fancy school. How was that?'

Hua Feng brightened slightly. 'Shanghai is so different from Cao Zhou. It is all hustle and bustle. And I'm studying German and medicine at Tongji University. It was set up by German doctors with a grant from the German government four years ago, but it's already packed full of students. It has all the modern western equipment and western knowledge.'

Chen smiled, but his eyes had a strange look to them. 'I thought for sure I would never see you again. You know . . . now that it seems like you'll be a commoner like just the rest of us. I figured you'd set off for Europe. That's why I was so surprised to hear of your engagement to Li.'

Hua breathed out and took a deep breath. 'To be honest, I would have loved to make a trip to the West. I've heard such amazing things from the doctors and the missionaries. I heard that they have railroads extending to every part of the country. They have markets with goods from every part of the world and zoos with animals from every corner of the earth. It all sounds so exotic . . . but my father made the arrangement with Li's father years ago. And since he passed not too long ago . . . I guess I felt like I must keep to his wishes.'

Chen's brow furrowed slightly, and he took a sip of his water cup, 'But since Li . . . since now the arrangement is off, you could go to the West. What brings you back to Mudan?'

'Isn't it obvious? I have come to investigate his murder and put to rest his vengeful spirit.'

Chen sprayed water across the table and began to choke. 'You are WHAT?' coughed Chen.

'You heard me. I am not that little noble girl you chased through the town, Chen. Shanghai is no peach, and I have grown up quite a bit in my time there.'

'No, no. No, no, no. NO,' Chen sputtered. 'Hua, these are not the kind of men you can deal with. I am the police force here. I will take care of the matter. Do not fret.'

Hua looked around the empty office. 'Chen . . . you don't even have an inkwell to go with your quill. How are you going to find the murderer?'

'Well, what about you then? How would you possibly help?'

'I am not without my connections, Chen. Plus, I have a secret weapon.'

'A what?'

'Never mind . . . tell me what you know? How was Li murdered?'

Chen rubbed his forehead exasperated, 'He was slashed across his chest. One long slash. His father as well. It seems like it must have been one killer—two at most— sneaking into the shop right before closing,' Chen took another gulp of water, 'Personally, I think it was the Gelaohui again. They must know that with the old deputy dead, we are sitting ducks.'

Hua turned and left abruptly.

'Hey! Hey, wait, Hua!' shouted Chen coming after her. 'Where are you going?'

'Think, Chen,' replied Hua, not slowing her pace. 'I am returning to the shop before they close. If it was the Gelaohui, then that means there would be things missing.'

'Ah,' Chen said with sudden realization. 'Ahhhhhh . . . that's a good idea Hua. Hey! Hey, wait up!'

* * *

'Nothing?'

'Nothing.'

'Not money? No wares? They took nothing?' questioned Hua with resolution.

'They took nothing,' repeated Granny Li firmly.

'Hmm.'

'Hmm?' repeated Chen, confounded. 'So . . . what does this mean?'

'Chen, this means that it wasn't the Gelaohui. Bandits are not going to come to kill two men, and then take nothing,' explained Hua Feng. 'This means that there was a different reason for the murders . . . possibly for personal reasons.'

Again, Hua Feng turned and left briskly without a word.

'So, where are we going now?' asked Chen panting as he caught up with Hua on the dark road heading out of town. Her getas seemed to fall heavily into the dirt road. It made Chen nervous.

'It is just a hunch, but I was a little disturbed by something that old man Wen said. Something about nobles and peasants not marrying . . .'

Chen halted at the thought, 'Hua, you can't be serious. Old man Wen couldn't hurt a fly. He barely leaves his farm as it is.'

Hua stopped. 'If Shanghai has taught me anything, it's that you never really know a person. Your best friend could turn around and stab you in the back. That is the way of the world, Chen. If you are going to wear that uniform and that topknot—then I suggest you recognize that.'

'Hush,' whispered Chen frantically.

'Don't tell me to hu—'

'Quiet! Look! A group of armed men are coming this way. You see those torches!'

* * *

The dozen or so men carried swords. Large swords. With long handles of equal length of their blades which were the size of a man's leg. They wore the modern shirts and pants of the Europeans, a dirty dark blue full of patches and holes. On their heads, half of them wore western-style hats made of straw and bale to keep cool from the blazing sun during the day. One man stood out from among the dark, plain-faced peasant-warriors. He had a round face with small dark eyes and a pair of thin lips tightly closed. He led them as they marched into town.

'Who are you?'

'Do not fear. I am the son of Mao Yichang, a peasant such as yourselves. I am here on orders of the Giutuo to protect you from a roving band of murderous Christians.'

Hua was about to open her mouth when Chen said, 'Ah yes! We were expecting you. I had completely forgotten.'

'You are the deputy, yes?'

Chen nodded.

'Why are you heading out of town?'

Hua began to speak when Chen interjected, 'This here. She is an old friend of mine. We are just going to see an old friend on his farm just outside of town. We won't be long.'

The round man had an ugly look on his face. Whether out of disgust or spite, Hua could not say. She looked at him up and down. He had skinny arms and short stubby legs. His chest was small with a protruding potbelly. Clasped to his chest with one small hand was a red book. This triggered a certain feeling in Hua.

What was it? Did I know this man? She thought to herself. Before she could say a word, the ugly man gave a curt nod and marched past them with his band.

'Hua? Hua, what is it?'

'Hmm? Nothing. Let's get moving . . . it looks like it is going to rain tonight.'

* * *

Old man Wen had lived in the same house as his father and his father's father before him. It was of the old style with slanted tiled roofs and bright red posts holding up a veranda all around the house. Surrounding the small house were dark green fields of recently harvested peony shrubs. The inner lamps were still brightly lit, illuminating the interior of the home. Old man Wen sat in his favourite chair by the firepit, smoking his favourite pipe and eating a bowl of rice. Hua sighed and entered through his front door roughly.

'WHO—oh, it's you, Junjun. You gave me quite a fright just now,' stated Wen, and then, upon seeing Chen, remarked puzzled, 'And deputy Chen, what are you both doing here so late?'

'We have some questions for you, Mr Wen, if you would be so kind,' said Chen not unkindly.

'Yes, of course . . . what kind of questions?' asked Wen, looking back and forth between the two.

'It is harvest time now, right?' asked Hua.

'Well, yes, Junjun, as you well know.'

'You have your reaper near?'

'Yes, just outside my side door,' replied Wen, confused.

'Could you go fetch it, please?'

'Certainly, princess.'

Old man Wen's knee joints cracked as he stood up, and his floor creaked as he walked to the side door and retrieved a large reaping scythe. He presented it to the two for inspection.

Wen shuffled his feet nervously. 'Would either of you like some rice? I've boiled it with my famous red peony sauce. It is the best around. It's like the wise philosopher used to say, "I eat nothing without its sauce. I enjoy it very much because of its flavour." It gives it a certain savoury flavour. I never forget to put it in with my rice. My sauce, that is. Ah, I make it with peony.' Hua continued to examine the blade of the scythe. 'Cáozhōu is—you know—the capital of peony. The peony, king of the flowers, flower of riches and honour. The peony is the national flower of the Qing, you see. It symbolizes honour, love, wealth, affection and nobility. Feminine beauty, too!

Eh, how could I forget that? We have been cultivating the flowers here for about 1,300 years. Thousands and thousands of hexagonal fields in every direction—just of the flowers, and as many varieties. You know—'

'Wen?' said Hua looking at him sharply.

'Ah, yes, princess?'

'Where were you six nights ago?'

'The nights of the murder?' asked Wen as his eyes bulged out of his sockets. 'I was, was right here—at my farm. I was reaping the harvest before the rains came. I knew the rains were coming, you know. You can see the droplets just beginning to fall, just now, you see.'

'Yes,' remarked Hua, still looking at old man Wen intently. 'Did you know that Li was actually murdered by being slashed?

'Ah,' swallowed Wen. 'No, princess, I did, ah, not know that.'

'Back at Granny Li's home, you said something. Do you recall?'

Wen shook his head furiously.

'You said that nobles and peasants shouldn't be marrying . . . how strongly do you feel that way?'

Wen paled at the implication. 'Junjun, I, ah, I mean, well, you see,' Wen stammered. 'What I meant to say was, I don't agree with it, but I would never do anything that would hurt you or anyone else. How foolish would that be? To bring disorder to try and maintain order. That just doesn't make any sense, princess!'

Hua Feng stared at Wen hard for a moment, and then breathed a sigh of relief. 'He is telling the truth.'

Everyone exhaled and there was a general lifting of tension in the room. The silence that followed was quickly followed by a loud rumbling and gurgling. Wen and Chen both looked at each other, and then stared at Hua. Hua's cheeks coloured and she simply said, 'Actually, Wen, I think I would love to have some of that famous rice with peony sauce, if you don't mind.'

Outside of old man Wen's, the rain fell at a light drizzle, slowly covering the ground and emitting the pleasant fragrance of wet earth and minty rose. The bright pink and dark rosy-coloured flowers glistened under the moonlight.

'Okay, Hua. I think that's enough for tonight,' stated Chen as he held the umbrella above Hua's head. 'I will walk you to your father's house at the other end of town and then, if you're going to insist on persisting in this folly, we can continue in the morning.'

Hua stopped.

'Why did you do it, Chen?'

Chen froze.

'What?' said Chen as he turned.

'Why did you kill him?'

'Hua . . . I never—'

'Don't lie to me, Chen!' said Hua, her voice quivering. 'You have the only other blade in town. You never liked Li. Admit it. You were always jealous, because . . . because you loved me!'

'I did love you, Hua,' said Chen. 'But I gave up on that ghost a long time ago. I wasn't happy you married Li. It was unfair after all. You rejected my proposal because you said you wanted a life outside of this little town—you said you wanted to see the world . . . and then you returned for him.'

The rain began to fall heavily. The hexagon of flowers became little islands in a muddy sea. Lightning flashed in the distance, lighting up the fields like pink and violet kaleidoscopes.

'But, Hua, my problem was never with Li. And I did not kill him,' Chen said with conviction.

'But, if not you, then—'

Lightning flashed again, and Hua saw the face of the ugly man before her eyes. Hua straightened her back when the truth dawned on her. 'The book!' she almost screamed. 'I know who did it! Quick, let's go!'

Chen followed Hua down the muddy path back to the city as she explained. 'The book. It's a western book. It's called *The Communist Manifesto* by a German philosopher. Li and his father were not killed because of who they were, but what they were!'

'What do you mean?'

'They were merchants, Chen. The leader of that group of Big Swords. He's a revolutionary. He must want to kill all the merchants in China. We have to find him!'

* * *

It didn't take long for Chen and Hua to catch up with the patrol in town. They were laughing amongst themselves on the other side of Li's shop under the eaves, drinking and smoking.

'You killed him!' screamed Hua Feng above the pouring rain. She raised an accusatory finger and pointed at the short leader.

'Hua, what are you doing?' whispered Chen frantically.

'I know what I am doing,' said Hua with determination.

'I don't know what you're talking about,' said the ugly man with a round face walking towards the couple with a sword in hand.

'My name is Hua Feng, daughter of Wang Feng, the former prefect of this district. I was betrothed under the heavens to Li Yen whom you murdered some days ago for no crime other than his occupation.'

'And so, what if I did? There are a million others just like him in this country. Bloodsucking tics! All of them! Leeching off on the labour of the proletariat. Making money off the backs of the working class. It makes me sick. We are doing something greater than you, stupid girl. If you don't like it, then you can run back to Tsingtao like the rest of the nobles and merchants. Rats and cockroaches. All of you! We are ushering in a new era!' the soldier with the round face shouted, raising his fist in the air. His black beady eyes flashed as he looked past Hua Feng towards something that only he could see.

'No!' retorted Hua Feng. 'His name was Li Yen, son of Li Soo. There was only one of him!' And in one swift motion, Hua opened her blue robe to reveal a musket in her hands.

The men of the Big Sword Society froze. The man with the beady eyes swallowed hard. 'Now be careful, girl. Be careful, you don't hurt yourself with that.'

'Oh, I wouldn't worry about myself,' replied Hua as she levelled the musket at the ugly man. The rain poured down hard and fast quickly creating a large, muddied puddle between the two.

She pulled the trigger.

Nothing happened!

'The flint! It's wet, boss. It won't fire.'

Hua Feng looked up wide-eyed at the men as grins spread across their faces.

'Get her!'

'I'm going to make her pay!'

'Quick!'

Lightning flashes struck the body of water between them. A foolhardy bandit had pre-emptively jumped towards Hua and he had been struck by a jolt as he put his foot in the water. He trembled and jerked about until he fell face first into the puddle.

The other men froze and looked at one another.

'Do not come forward!' screamed a voice from behind Hua.

Hua turned to see Granny Li coming towards the group with her large, bright yellow lantern in hand.

'Do you not see the bad luck at work here! Lightning has struck between you. Only misfortune will come upon you if you dare cross this line. Flee. FLEE!' And at that, the men turned around and ran. Only the son of Mao Yichang hesitated. He gave one last dark look at Hua with his black eyes, and then finally left for good.

For the longest minute, Hua just stared at the fleeing soldiers as they faded into the dark. Then, Hua sank to her knees and wept.

'There, there, Hua. You did what you could do. Li Yen's spirit is at peace that we all know his murderer's face. That is enough. That is enough. There is nothing else you could do.'

Granny Li and Chen helped Hua Feng inside as the rain continued to pour down upon the little town of Cao Zhou that fateful night.

The Himachal Leopard

Keith Peter Jardim

for Isabella, Natalia and Alex—new in the world

> *He who sees himself in all beings,*
> *And all beings in him,*
> *Attains the highest Brahman,*
> *Not by any other means.*

> — Kaivalya Upanishad

That first morning on the large balcony in the Himalayan summer light, Jerry knew it would be foolish to say anything about what Surinder had told him of the night leopard. He was having breakfast with his parents, whose behaviour so far today had been exemplary. The voices of twenty-five other hotel guests sitting as couples or in small family groups under sun-umbrellas were hushed by the vast array of snow-dappled mountains to the north and a sky so luminous and dark blue it seemed weighted in place by its colour. His father, Henry Blythe, was reading the *Times of India*, and his mother, Jean, was buttering her naan bread. Jerry mused on what the day would bring. He was hoping to meet Surinder later. And Manpreet, where was she? Would he see her again? Jerry had never met anyone like her.

His father, stern and edgy when they had arrived from Chandigarh after a five-hour drive yesterday afternoon, was annoyed at the location of the hotel—further away from Shimla than he had thought.

'Why the deception?' he had asked Jerry's mother in the lobby. 'The damn Internet was useless. Why couldn't I get a simple answer to a straight question?'

Jerry's mother had turned from the receptionist to Henry, her patience wearing thin, Jerry saw, and said, 'Because English is different everywhere now and you know that. Remember Lisbon last year? Relax, dear. Look at the hotel! Why would we ever want to leave?'

'For what they charged at that Lisbon hotel, everyone there should have spoken fluent English!'

'Henry, the world—'

His parents had continued to bicker, his mother soon raising her voice to challenge his father's. To Jerry, this behaviour, more frequent in recent years, had occasionally felt like acting, as if they were rehearsing for a play he had no knowledge of.

In the midst of their exchange, two porters had brought in their bags on a trolley and whisked them off to an elevator. Their movements and the trolley's made no sound on the multi-rugged floor, an elaborate selection of Persian design— bright reds, creams, yellows, blacks and greens hypnotizing in their patterns and geometric precision. To the left of the entrance was a large sitting area of pale lime-green sofas, beige cushioned chairs, and coffee tables. Tall, immaculately clean French casement windows showed the driveway and a croquet-set lawn beyond. At the far end of the room was the biggest fireplace Jerry had ever seen; and above it, framed in gold fretwork, his dour gaze missing nothing of Henry and Jean Blythe's performance, was the portrait of Lord Kitchener.

Right when Jerry thought he would run out of the lobby from embarrassment and across the lawn to the tall blue pine and deodar trees where a path led deep into a dark-green forest, a young woman appeared in a blue and lavender sari, her belly button visible, black eyes piercing and concerned, lustrous abundant black hair elegantly arranged around her neck and the back of her head. She smiled beautifully at them, and Jerry was struck by her real, well-formed eyebrows. She lifted the tray of three drinks she was carrying and said, her melodious voice soothing them with the same emotion as her eyes, 'Something bad is happening? I have delayed the complimentary welcome drinks! I am very sorry. Please forgive me and accept my offer of free dinner any night you wish in our dining room.'

Thankfully, his parents had stopped their squabbling and accepted the drinks, and nodding and smiling at the young woman, sipped them. Then, she came to Jerry and offered his drink, he shyly lowering his gaze for her face was a dazzle of charm and impish beauty, her smile as natural as morning light.

'Mister . . . Jerry?' she said softly, dipping her head to the side and looking up at him to catch his eyes, which were focused on her aquamarine blue toenails. She wore leather-soled sandals, the tops of her feet and toes bare except for the thin straps from toe to heel. She wiggled her toes and Jerry, blushing and smiling, looked at her. He took his drink off the tray she held to him.

'Keep this drink with juniper-berry flavour our little secret. It is a very weak one.' She winked her right eye.

'You know my name—'

'Registration form, of course,' she said quickly, as if not wanting him to endure any more discomfort. 'You are eighteen, but not married yet,' she giggled. Then, in a fervent whisper, 'That is wise!'

'Jerry?' his mother called. 'Room sixty-five, sixth floor, whenever you're ready.'

His parents seemed oddly at peace now. His father was even smiling at him. What mood swings they were having these days!

His mother raised a hand and waved, saying, 'Thank you, Miss . . . err?'

'I am begging your pardon, madam. My name is Manpreet.' She had swung around to face his parents, and her hair, the sheer weight of it, shifted. Jerry got a faint whiff of cedar.

His father, looking faintly amused now, asked, 'Does that mean something?'

'Oh, yes,' Manpreet laughed, scratching the side of her head. 'It means "mind full of love".'

'How very interesting,' said Jerry's mother.

His parents, now at the elevators, both watched Jerry and Manpreet, his mother a little anxious, he thought, her mouth tensing.

Manpreet had faced him again and was recommending a meeting with Surinder as soon as possible. And yes, she told him, continuing to address the activities and questions he had filled out and answered on the hotel's website, there

were one or two leopards around, something she hoped he
would keep quiet.

'You've researched videos on the Internet?'

Jerry sipped his drink nervously and confessed he had.
And what a drink it was: he loved berries, and the other
thing, the secret ingredient, which was gin, he knew, was a
surprise. That was two secrets already. He was beginning to
wonder about Manpreet. Then she had led him outside and
introduced him to Surinder, the forest guide and a retired
zoologist although he was no older than Jerry's father. He
greeted Jerry enthusiastically, his jowly cheeks trembling
a little. He had thinning silvery hair, but was well-muscled
and fit. Immediately, he began telling Jerry about the summer
school in life sciences he ran in Shimla. Then Manpreet, after
speaking rapidly in Hindi to Surinder, had smiled at them
both, but in particular at Jerry, her smile warming a part of his
upper chest and neck, and left as abruptly as she had appeared.

* * *

As he ate his *gobi ka paratha* and eggs with buttered wheat
toast, Jerry wondered who, or what exactly, had deceived his
father. One of the headlines on the *Times of India* front page
was 'Tensions Continue to Rise on Sino-Indian Border'.

'Oh-ho, listen to this,' Mr Blythe grunted, folding and
rustling the large pages of the *Times of India*, and then reaching
for his coffee.

'Well? What is it now? Another skirmish on the border?'
His mother bit into a scone and peered at her husband as
he sipped his coffee. Late last night from their hotel room,
they all three had seen five soldiers patrolling the surrounding
gardens. By daylight, they were gone.

'Worse,' his father said. 'And closer.'

Jerry knew what was coming. Surinder had told him.

'"Leopard kills 74-year-old in Kinnaur". That's about eighty-five miles from here.'

'The soldiers were way closer last night,' Jerry said.

Here, Mr Blythe scrutinized his son's face over the top of the newspaper, then he began reading.

'"A leopard killed a 74-year-old woman of Ribba village in Kinnaur district in the wee hours of Sunday. The victim has been identified as Lapsar Devi. The incident has created panic in the area as the woman was sleeping inside her room when the leopard pounced on her. The administration has instructed police and forest officials to kill the animal which is now targeting villagers. Leopard attacks have killed nine people in the Kinnaur and Rampur areas so far. As per sources, the leopard entered the house after breaking the door and attacked Lapsar Devi at midnight when her family was sleeping in another room. It dragged her to a nearby field some 200 metres from the house. As dogs started barking, the leopard ran away leaving the woman critically injured."'

'Still want to be a zoologist?' Jerry's father asked him.

'Poor woman,' Mrs Blythe shook her head. 'Wonder what her name means.'

'More than ever, dad,' Jerry said and slipped his phone out of his shirt pocket and typed in the woman's name. 'It means fallen heavenly goddess, Mum. Devi means divine, anything of excellence; Lapsar seems related to lapsarian. Lapsed.'

'Hear that, Henry? English comes from all over the place; it's quite fascinating.'

Jerry looked at his father, who frowned at them both and went back to his reading.

Mrs Blythe leaned forward to her son as he read from his phone. Then, she looked north to the Greater Himalayas in the far distance, their icy-blue peaks like surf against the ocean of sky. In the suite last night, she and Jerry had read a brochure describing several of the higher mountains, all ranging from 4,500 to 5,600 metres, their names like remnants of a lost ancient poem: Kangla, Baralacha, Parang and Pin Parvati. It was the beginning of the edge of the world, he felt, a place of grave beauty and last things.

'We're on holiday, Henry. Leave Jerry alone.'

Jerry took his glass of orange juice and drank it all in one go. He sighed, waiting for his father's reply and another useless, irritating debate about his future. He decided to excuse himself and was about to rise and return to the little room he fortunately had to himself through a door in his parents' suite, when they heard a voice, a sound of mountain light so sweet and lucid it might be the voice of the goddess Devi herself speaking from the top of the world.

'The ultimate reality is a goddess, says the Devisukta: "I have created all worlds at my will without being urged by any higher Being, and dwell within them. I permeate the earth and heaven, and all created entities with my greatness and dwell in them as eternal and infinite consciousness." And Nanda Devi, meaning "bliss-giving goddess", is named after her, such a mysterious place and not so very far from here . . .'

Manpreet wore jeans and a loose black shirt, the sleeves rolled to her elbows. Her long black hair was coiffed in a big tight bun with a cedar-spike. Jerry thought it must be full of secrets. Her beautiful dark eyebrows were slightly quizzical, inquiring. And already at this hour, there was a mischievous glint in her eyes. His heart lifted.

'And how is the family doing this morning?' she asked, standing next to Jerry's chair and placing her hand atop its back.

Mr Blythe had put down his newspaper and was scrutinizing her too.

'You look very different today,' he said.

'New day, new responsibilities,' Manpreet laughed. 'We're all the time busy here, even in the off-season, which really, now I think about it, we do not have.'

'I see,' Mr Blythe said.

'Is it possible to visit Nanda Devi?' asked Jerry. He leaned back slightly in his chair to address her, and suddenly felt her fingers on the back of his neck. She did not move her hand. Jerry watched his mother to see if she had noticed.

'I've read about the Nanda Devi incident,' Mrs Blythe said. 'That was quite a misadventure.'

'There's a story that went too far,' Mr Blythe said.

His parents sounded as if they were speaking from a shared experience, but it was before their time. Jerry had skimmed a lengthy article on the Internet about the Nanda Devi plutonium incident.

Manpreet sighed. 'Yes, a sad story, like all stories if they go along far enough. I'm afraid no visiting is allowed, Jerry. And it is quite far. The Sanctuary Park is possible. But why go all the way there when so much is here?'

Manpreet waved her other hand at the view. The back of Jerry's neck was getting warm.

'You're right,' Jerry said, feeling his chest pulse with blood.

'I see,' Mr Blythe said.

Jerry's mother glared at her husband. Jerry looked off at the mountains.

'You're so very right, Mr Blythe, about stories. My cousin is thinking of suicide since her fiancé broke off their engagement. It is most regretful. I've done all I can to persuade her to live, but, I don't know. Maybe she should have left the relationship when they were at best, then perhaps—oh, who knows when their story should have ended. But they all end somehow, sometime. Don't they?'

Jerry's mother was staring at Manpreet, her mouth half-open during this revelation. Manpreet had gently removed her hand while speaking from the back of Jerry's chair, her thumb quickly secretly caressing his upper spine as she stepped to the midway point of the circular umbrella-shaded table, to stand between Jerry and his father. His father picked up his newspaper, pointing to the story of the leopard.

'Is it true what I've heard about the problems of relocating leopards? Is this an example? I'm wondering if this story may have been a result of bad decisions.' He handed Manpreet the newspaper.

Jerry's mother rolled her eyes, saying, 'Henry, a little sympathy, please! I'm sorry to hear about your cousin, Manpreet. I hope she gets better and makes the right decision. So many young people are ending their lives these days, everywhere. Very unfortunate.'

'Most certainly it is, Mrs Blythe. Maybe the cause comes from—' she flicked a hand upward and outward at the mountains, her graceful fingers enacting a deft dance-like movement, her nails a spruce-green—'not worshipping the right things. Mountains, for instance! The preservation of the Himalaya environment has now become one of India's top priorities.'

A cool wind drifted across the beige-tiled, sunlit balcony. The frilly saffron, blue and yellow cotton balls decorating the umbrellas' edges stirred and Jerry saw a light strand of

Manpreet's hair loosen across her ear. Her cedar perfume came to him again, this time with a faint touch of vanilla. The umbrellas' shadows were shorter.

Manpreet glanced at the story of the leopard. 'Yes, Mr Blythe, I believe it is possible this is a relocation problem. They are nearly all going wrong, in so many ways too.' She gave a weary smile and handed the newspaper back. 'Those relocations are all going to stop soon, I am hoping, at least in our Himachal area. Surinder is working on it.'

Mr Blythe cleared his throat and said, 'I will give you fifteen-hundred pounds if you persuade my son, the only child I have, to realize the dangers of becoming a zoologist and pick another career.'

She replied immediately, even before Mrs Blythe had time to recover, as if she had been expecting his proposal. 'Such a career is not really dangerous for Jerry, Mr Blythe. And I am very well-employed with the hotel, sir. Your offer is one I cannot accept, under any circumstances.' She placed her hands together as if in prayer and bowed a little, her face a mask of aloof civility.

'Henry!' Jerry's mother shouted. 'What an absolutely outrageous thing to say! Have you no manners at all? No consideration for the young lady? For your son?'

His parents began to argue. Jerry stood up and looked helplessly at Manpreet.

'Follow me,' she said.

They left walking fast and close, their arms brushing against each other and went up the short flight of steps in the brilliant summer light and into the hotel's Jawaharlal Nehru dining area and through it toward the lobby and outside to the croquet-set lawn, where Manpreet began explaining when Jerry asked about the Nanda Devi, Indian Defence Force,

CIA-spying incident against China and the pollution from the plutonium device. It had almost started another war. He was watching her as much as possible, trying his best not to trip and fall. They hiked up and up through the forest of cypress, deodar and blue pine toward Surinder's Leopard Lookout, as he called it, Manpreet slowing the pace once they were beyond sight of the hotel. In the shade of the tall trees, the morning was still fresh and cool. The staccato warning from a scimitar-babbler trickled among the trees alerted Jerry and concerned, he looked at Manpreet. She laughed, reassuring him that leopards hunt mostly at night, right after dusk. As if you didn't know! The loosened strand of her hair he had noticed at breakfast lifted again in a drift of mountain air, curling across her ear. He had a sharp urge to reach out and tuck it into her heavy bun.

'Your hair must be very long,' he said.

'Not so much.' She gave him a searching look like the one yesterday afternoon in the lobby, but this time it meant something different; her eyes had narrowed slightly. He felt himself blush and she looked away, smiling a little.

'Do you always wear it up?'

'Usually. It is still frowned upon in certain parts for an unmarried woman to wear it long. Or so I've been warned.' She laughed. 'But the only warnings I really listen to are those Surinder tells me about leopards.'

'A wise move,' he said, hoping his face was no longer red. He looked ahead, up the path; there was sunlight streaming down on the ground here and there, and above it, the trees swayed in a gentle wind.

'What do your parents do?'

'You mean apart from annoying each other?' He laughed. 'They work together, which probably explains a lot. Consultants. Diplomacy, politics, public relations with these huge multinational corporations. They want me to follow in their footsteps, but my mum is less insistent.'

He was reluctant to continue.

'Surinder told me you have a passion for feline study. Like him. I have always wondered where it comes from. I would like to pursue it myself. Do you think we are people who want to be cats, a leopard perhaps?'

Jerry nodded. 'I think there's something in that. Surinder said yesterday that the human relationship with big cats is hundreds of thousands of years old and complicated, especially with leopards. Our evolution was assisted by leopards, he said. I never would have thought that.'

'Oh, yes. Their intelligence, the way they adapt, in order to survive is unique. They keep improving their chances of survival, especially in India. Did you see the Internet video of a leopard at night walking up a secured driveway to the main entrance door, where a dog is sleeping on the welcome mat? I could not believe it.'

Jerry was grinning. 'Amazing,' he said. 'It was incredible how close the leopard put his head to the dog's, just looking at it from a couple inches away, waiting and waiting for it to wake up. For at least ten minutes! At first, I thought something was wrong with the video because the leopard was so still. Nothing moved.'

'Then the dog wakes up and barks, hysterical. The leopard picks him up and off they go. The men come out of the door and chase. The leopard let the dog go, that was smart. He knew something was not right about it.'

'Everything,' and he looked at her.

Manpreet gave him a sad smile. 'There is hope, Jerry. The leopards are getting smarter, and even appear to cooperate in certain situations. Humans, well . . . not so much. But more people are learning, just not quickly enough.' She sighed.

'Sometimes I think they think we are undeserving of this world. The Rudraprayag man-eater killed over one hundred and fifty. And there is another leopard of legend, a female, she killed over four hundred supposedly. So many other man-eaters, leopards, lions and tigers. But the leopard is supreme. As if it were chosen for the task of—'

'Communication, to deliver a message to us?'

'Exactly! But Waghoba can achieve cooperation that reduces violence between leopards and humans.'

Jerry's phone pinged and he glanced at it. 'Mum. She's wondering where we are. Return time.'

'In two hours we return, in time for lunch. Surinder will bring us.'

He tapped his phone a few times. Then, with the phone still in his hand, he looked at her, slowing his walk. A few yards ahead of him, she paused and turned. 'You want a picture of me?'

'Since yesterday.' He was surprised at his own confidence and didn't trust it.

'Oh?' Manpreet smiled, considering him. Her right hand rose to the back of her head, stayed there. 'You want to see my hair?'

'Oh, yes. First up, then down, please?'

She laughed. 'That's life in the mountains. And every day with my hair.'

Manpreet stood in a beam of sunlight. On the count of three, he took the first picture, her face still thoughtful, also amused now. As she was taking her hair down, removing the cedar-spike, he touched the record button with his thumb, longing for more than just the memory of her voice and movement. Her black hair fell wide and thick to her waist on her front and sides, the mass and gloss of it shaking like something alive, febrile.

Then she removed her phone and took a series of rapid photos of him.

Jerry stopped recording and looked at her. She took two steps toward him. And another. 'Thank you,' he said.

Manpreet stood a metre from him, looking into his eyes. 'You are most welcome.'

He knew he should kiss her, but he was nervous and felt his blush returning. When she looked down and away to the left in the direction they had come from, he was sure she was embarrassed for him. Jerry looked at her sneakers. Right there, between his feet and hers, he saw the first pugmark. Then another.

'Look!' Manpreet said, still watching the direction from where they had come. Jerry followed her gaze; where the ground was soft, there were occasional pugmarks, no doubt those of a leopard. In unison, their heads swung uphill, and then they began to follow the tracks slowly. They photographed them often for Surinder who, Manpreet said, would be able to identify more about them. Another fifty yards up the hill, the pugmarks went off the path into the forest.

'How recent do you think they are?' he asked her.

Manpreet was serious and distracted; she was walking quickly. 'Ah, I think last night. This could be very important. We must get to Surinder fast.'

* * *

The Leopard Lookout was a rickety hut above an apple orchard that sloped down to a valley with emerald-green paddy fields. From their position, they could see much of the Himachal hill country rising north to the snow-mountains.

Forest, orchards and rice paddies bordered each other almost everywhere, and the escarpments were sunlit and shaded blue in the late morning distances. A few miles to the west, parts of Shimla lay obscured by haze, as if teetering on the mountainsides. The morning had remained clear away from the city. It was cooler here. The hut stood in shadows among a grove of deodar and blue pine. The door was shut. Manpreet knocked on it and Surinder said, 'Come in.'

I should have kissed her, Jerry thought. *I'm a fool. I should have kissed her and kissed her and kissed her.*

Surinder was sitting at a small wooden table looking at his phone. He wore a green sweater, khaki trousers and black sneakers. Manpreet lifted her phone to him as he looked up at them. 'You saw them too,' he said, sadly. 'Glad you're keeping an eye out, Manpreet. I wouldn't want you two to miss out on what is really happening around here. Especially with the army roaming all over the place.'

Jerry looked at Manpreet, then Surinder. The honk-like alarm call of a sambar deer came through the trees. Then, once more.

'And soon, the *kakar* will bark,' said Surinder.

'A leopard is near,' said Manpreet.

Surinder held up his phone to them. 'A leopard is always close by in these mountains, but that's our secret. Look at these photos, and then at those on your phone. Tell me if you notice anything. A hint: these are not the pugmarks of the hotel leopard that passes near the guard hut thrice a month, at night.'

Jerry again noticed the sadness in his voice. They both studied the pugmark photos on Surinder's phone, Jerry watching Manpreet's face for a clue as to what this lesson was about. But she was distracted, almost irritable, he thought. 'Where are yours from?' she asked.

'Aha, that's my student! The first good question. These pugmarks are from Kinnaur, sent to me by Digvijay three days ago. Jerry, what do you think?'

'Are you suggesting these pugmarks are from the same leopard whose pugmarks we photographed a short while ago?'

'I am indeed. It is quite possible.'

'Our Lord Shiva, the old man returned!' exclaimed Manpreet. 'More proof that relocation is point—' instantly her enthusiasm ceased. She looked at Jerry. Her face and shoulders slumped. 'Where in Kinnaur district did Digvijay take the photos?'

Surinder lowered his head, almost on the verge of tears, 'Ribba village.'

Manpreet flung a look heavenward, '*Maadher-chod*, Shiva!'

Surinder raised a hand. 'Take it easy, now, behave. I'm not yet sure why this relocation happened.'

'But we damn well know who's to blame: Government reservation bureaucrats! What are the odds that it is Shiva?'

'"What" is to blame,' Surinder corrected. 'Never "who". It is behaviour. Human behaviour . . . which can be changed. Remember that, always. If you cannot, then there is no hope. That it's Shiva is very likely, I'm afraid.'

Jerry sensed a magisterial patience in the man. It was stronger than his sadness.

Manpreet clasped her hands behind her head and paced the confines of the hut, taking slow, deep breaths. 'Yes,' she said mournfully. 'Hope. It has brought us all this far. The story of hope! A very human story. The eternal one! Maybe it has come to its end. If so, there is only one place left to go now, and that is up.'

She stood in the far corner of the hut, arms folded, looking out through a narrow rectangular opening.

Surinder groaned. 'You think such talk is helping Jerry?'

Manpreet turned from the window and looked at them, the right side of her face was lit by the sun; a fugitive fury lay there. 'He's old enough to hear that. And much more. And, Surinder, let me ask you: What in hell is going to change human behaviour in time, before the ecosystems and their inhabitants are all gone? Then what happens? We all march up to the Himalaya summits, wearing oxygen masks, and cavort with the remaining wildlife?'

'Good questions, indeed!' Surinder raised his palms to the hut's ceiling, and then placed them on his ageing head. 'But I want you both to learn this: it's wrong to blame people, because the moment we start doing that, we get on the road to conflict. The record of that is long and depressing, Manpreet, you know it. Now, as soon as we can document this case, we'll have more proof that leopard relocation is not working. It'll help. You see, Jerry, Waghoba is the only hope. And the leopards are learning it. Did Manpreet tell you?'

Jerry nodded vigorously, hoping somehow to calm Manpreet.

'Relocation failure may make them think killing leopards will work even better,' Manpreet said. 'They won't bother with Waghoba like the others. Too primitive, they think. The little education they received has made them all monsters. They hang it on the wall and make it a decoration. It's not even educa—'

'Stop it!' Surinder slammed his palms down on the table.

Jerry jumped. He felt he should do something, say something. He was about to ask if Waghoba was being taught in any government schools when a hollow-sounding bark drew their attention. Instantly, the mood in the hut shifted; Manpreet walked quickly to the door and opened it an inch to look out. Surinder got up and tapped his phone a few times. Jerry removed his phone. Manpreet did not touch hers.

'Was that the kakar?' whispered Jerry.

The bark came again, more resonant this time, closer. Surinder came to the door, looking at Jerry and smiling through his sadness. 'Let us hope the kakar is saying 'beast', and not man.'

'Beast,' Manpreet said, and rushed from the door—the young woman she was moments before gone as she sang, 'My lord. My sweet . . . lord.'

Jerry stepped toward the door and Surinder grabbed his arm. 'Wait. You cannot go out. Even I can only stand in the doorway. When I step out, you open the door a little. You will see such a sight!—one you will never forget. But whatever you do, make no sound, no moves. And do not tell a soul what you see. All will be explained in due course. You promise?'

'I promise,' said Jerry.

* * *

Dinner, Jerry admitted to himself as he ate, was extremely good. At first, he had thought Manpreet might express disapproval about his chosen dish of venison, which was his favourite meat; but she had grinned happily at his choice. And when he said medium-well was how he liked it, she suggested the meat would be better a little less cooked, with a bit more blood. 'It really brings out the flavour—not just of the earth, but of life itself,' said Manpreet.

Mrs Blythe had given her a quick, sharp look.

They had, that afternoon after the incident at Leopard Lookout with Surinder, developed an efficient and artful way of communicating with each other around people; it sometimes involved words of seemingly meaningless observations or questions; also, there were slight shifts of the eyes, the lips, the nose, like twitching and mild sniffing. Or indicating something, or a direction, by pointing the nose and pinioning it with a basilisk stare for several seconds. Leopards and tigers, Surinder had said, use such communication, nose-pointing and staring by tigers especially because of their weak sense of smell. They had a proposal for his parents regarding Jerry attending the summer school, and both Surinder and Manpreet had advised him on the best method for a positive outcome. After that, they could only hope. His parents had ordered the *rogan josh* lamb curry and were extremely pleased with it.

'I quite like her,' Mrs Blythe said, 'I really do, Jerry, but she is very, very odd.'

'Yes,' he said smiling at his mother who, he noted, had been making a genuine effort for a pleasant evening. Much hope rested with her. 'She certainly is, but when you get to know her a bit, it's all perfectly in line with a sound ethical stance.'

His father looked up from the wine list, glasses about to slip over his nose. 'Hmm. In light of that, I'm surprised she seemed so pleased with your meaty appetite.'

'Completely unpredictable,' Jerry said. 'But, meat on occasion is an important part of the diet of many creatures, even us. The problem is, there are too many of us and we eat too much of it. Surinder is a master diplomat. He even runs a deer breeding farm not far from here,' Jerry pointed at his plate, 'lets them into the wild too. That way, the leopards have more choices and kill less livestock. I've never met anyone so patient, so interested in harmony. Balance. He would be a great partner in your consultancy work. He's the perfect teacher. I've learnt a lot from their discussions.'

His father gave him one of his scrutinizing looks. Jerry was pushing his luck, he knew. Relax, he thought. *Relax.*

'Are you in love, Jerry?' his mother asked.

'Maybe with leopards. After what I saw today . . .' He shut up.

His father chuckled. 'Well, my boy, you had that coming, didn't you? We've been here not even two days, and already so much is happening. No wedding plans, I hope. Now Jean, do you think the thin air is getting to him?'

Mrs Blythe managed to smile warmly at her husband. 'I'll think about that later, if need be, dear.'

'What did you see today?' Mr Blythe asked, his attention suddenly switching from Jerry to the high windows of the dining-room and the garden beyond.

In the dim lavender light, tinting well-ordered flowerbeds of blue poppies and meadow primroses, the Blythe family saw two officers of the Indian army strolling with someone who appeared to be the hotel manager. A few of the diners near the Blythes' table noticed the officers as well. Soon, there were murmurs throughout the dining room.

'Bang, bang!' a small boy yelled at a table near the dining-room entrance. Jerry stared at the child. Immediately, his mother quietened him. His father, a large man with thick black hair and large, black-rimmed glasses, was looking outside at the officers who descended the far side of the garden with the manager and disappeared. A noticeable unease bristled among the diners.

'We live in interesting times,' Mr Blythe said.

Mrs Blythe nodded, almost on cue, Jerry thought. Then she said, 'I wonder, dear, how many soldiers we'll have on patrol tonight.'

There was a restrained, polite 'good evening' behind Jerry's left shoulder. From the moment he saw Manpreet and Surinder, he knew the plan was postponed, for now. Maybe forever, depending on the armies in the region. As Surinder introduced himself to his parents, she twitched her nose at Jerry to confirm, and gave a three-second unblinking stare to where the officers and the hotel manager had been moments before.

I wonder, dear, how many soldiers we'll have on patrol tonight.

Blood surged to his neck, chest, arms and legs. A black-red rage.

Manpreet stepped close to his chair, rested a hand on his shoulder and pressed; Surinder was to her front, blocking his parents' view, but Jerry could see part of his father. Taking short, quick breaths, he drove from his mind the obscene image of himself leaping across the table and stabbing his father through the heart with his steak knife.

The cedar-vanilla perfume of her by his side, the feel of her hand still on his shoulder, and now, as she bent to him, a whisper of lines from a song—or was it a poem or a prayer—softly worded, perhaps softly written a millennium ago, calmed him.

While Surinder exchanged pleasantries with them and talked about the life-sciences summer institute he ran for high-school juniors, seniors, first-degree university students and older adults in nearby communities, including his plans for expanding and reinventing Waghoba, Jerry decided he would stay and attend the courses, no matter what. He would offset the cost by working in whatever way he could. To hell with his parents and their armies, their greed, their distortions and destructions.

Manpreet put a small note next to his plate. She pressed his shoulder again, and he felt the heat in her hand as he read:

. . . but there's no cage to him
More than to the visionary his cell:

His stride is wildernesses of freedom:
The world rolls under the long thrust of his heel.
Over the cage floor the horizons come.

* * *

Lord Shiva was tired, yet he ascended higher and higher.
At 5,200 metres, he could feel his spotted coat beginning to
thicken, his blood warming him. It was so far a first response
to the new climate after a two-day journey—reassuring, but
not enough. There was also hunger now, as vast as the Thar
Desert in Rajasthan. He would eat anything he wished; it
was permitted. The snow leopards had allowed him generous
passage. They knew.

Last night, the hiss and roar of two iron-birds as they wove
their perverted flight towards the Trishul and Nanda Devi
had terrorized him. They had killed their prey from above and
had neglected it; some they even cooked with fire and smoke,
and still, they did not descend to eat. It made no sense. Lord
Shiva had walked among their burnt prey; some were soldiers,
and some were not. He had bitten into one of them, eaten
just enough. Flesh like the pig; he preferred bharal with their
blue-tinted coats, but there were few of them here now.

The voice of the woman who had found him and saved
him when he was a cub was still in his head from two days
ago: the joy of it, the sound of untrammelled, Himalayan blue.
She was his sky and mountain forest. My Lord. My sweet! . . .
she had said and stroked his head and ears just the way he
loved and eventually he nudged her to the ground and she
bent her arms back and held her elbows firm as he rubbed his
back and flanks along them. His deep throat-rumbling and
half-closed eyes made her eyes wet.

The man had watched, as he had before, keeping his distance although he was closer than he had been in the past, trust having been established over time. Lord Shiva knew he was good. Then he had seen a bit of the face of another man, unfamiliar, behind him; a different kind of man—young. But her voice and eyes, after she looked back at the men, promised him all was well. There was nothing to fear. Not then.

The woman had stood, patting her shoulders with her arms crossed. Lord Shiva had reared up on his hind legs to rest his paws on her shoulders, slipping them around her as she hugged him, her face in his neck, his chest against hers, her head of hair, thick and long like the snow leopards', nuzzling his jaw.

'Go high, my Lord,' she had said. 'Go up to Nanda Devi, to the Trident. Find a cave. At night, look at the stars and think of me.'

She had pointed, making sure he understood, in the direction of the Sanctuary. The sound of her voice, a music of affection edged with tense concern, told him the rest.

Lord Shiva went higher and higher, onward to the edge of the world.

And the Crocodiles Lurk Below

Ismim Putera

'*Misi*! Misi!'

'*Apa?*' I asked the men.

'*Penghulu mau jumpa!*' they replied hastily, begging me to come down from my quarters.

A woman in a longhouse had been in labour for about two days. The midwives had summoned rainforest gods and mangrove spirits in propitiation. They had done everything they could. It was up to me to help her. Without wasting another minute, I put on my uniform and packed the 'delivery equipment' in a bag.

The river was serene. Nipa palms on the riverbanks, flanking the river with their serrated leaves, swayed gracefully in the water. The towering pedada trees stood firm like sentinels guarding the banks of the river. A crescent moon, like the grin of a Cheshire cat, guided us into the darkness as our *perahu* skied down the Rajang current.

The longhouse was built uphill along the riverbank, bounded by coconut trees. A row of kerosene lamps illuminated the indoor compartment. The flames glittered like fireflies when seen from afar.

'Oi! oi!' I turned to look at my Kayan friends. One of them was pointing towards the water.

'*Boyak*! Boyak!' he screamed.

'A crocodile?' I withdrew my hands from the hull and looked at the river. The water was unusually still. There was scarcely a ripple, as if time feared the creature too.

'Oi, oi, oi!' I heard more shouts from the men in the longhouse. They tried to pinpoint to us the location of the crocodile with their sharp eyes, but we had no idea where to look for it. It was dark and the air was dank. I failed to distinguish a thumb from an index finger on my hands!

'Don't move that way. The crocodile is on the other side of the boat!' shouted a man with a sword in each hand. He was handsomely robed with a headdress embellished with tufts of protruding hornbill feathers.

'Ohaaa! Ohaaa!' howled the man. His undeviating sight marked a spot on the water, revealing the hideous creature. It was twice the size of our skinny perahu. From under the dark water, it leered at us with a pair of greenish-yellow eyes, flashing moonlight glints like two floating golden orbs.

'Misi, *lompat dulu*! Lompat!' Someone grabbed my arm and guided me towards the stern as our perahu docked at the jetty. Another man tied the rope to moor the boat. Curiosity did kill the cat. I turned my head and accidentally made eye contact with the crocodile. It read the fear grating on my knees.

The animal thrust its cylindrical body towards us, as swift as an arrow, with a wake of sheets of blackish water. Its mouth was wide enough to swallow the whole perahu!

'Proooom . . . Prooom!' The strikes sent out a series of shock waves making us tremble as we stood on the sides of the perahu. 'Lompat!' We jumped out from the perahu and ran along the jetty to the longhouse. My sweat glands had even run out of sweat to drench myself. From the distance, we watched; the crocodile was determinedly dismantling the perahu into its elemental components. It was greyish black with thick, studded scales on its back. After a while, the crocodile slapped back into the water with a sound like a cannon shot.

* * *

The man with the traditional outfit was Penghulu Ranang, the chieftain of the longhouse. He assisted me to ascend the stairs into the longhouse. The longhouse was as tall as the coconut tree. I bowed my body and walked along the aisle bounded by men, women and naked children. I entered the labour room and introduced myself to no less than a dozen women in it, who were expecting my arrival.

The incident with the crocodile was abruptly flushed out of my mind.

I approached the distressed woman. She was supported by two elderly women and her limp hands held on to a rattan rope suspended above her. In less than two minutes, she gave her feedback to the list of pertinent questions, before I outlined my management plan. It seemed that she was a twenty-five-year-old primigravida with no previous surgical operation or medical illnesses. She had been having contractions for the past three days. By now, the pain was rather intense and came at shorter intervals. She had weakened considerably through vomiting several times that evening.

I made her lie down despite protests from the other women. I implored the ladies to heed the voice of reason and not blindly follow some weird taboos.

Among the anxious women, one appeared to be indifferent unlike the others. Her name was Lana. She was also the only one who understood Malay. She was a skinny midwife, in her late forties, and appeared rather authoritative. Many women had thanked her for pulling them through childbirth. She had grown rich and to display it, she wore heavy-looking, beaded necklaces around her neck, a pair of golden hoop earrings, brass bangles on both her wrists and I assumed, she had jungle produce in many jars, and coops with many fowls.

Lana, too, stood by unhappily. '*Kenak*? Kenak?' she questioned me repetitively.

'She must lie down properly. This is tiring!'

I was too busy to explain to her. Instead, I quickly examined the woman and manually counted the foetal heartbeats using a Pinard stethoscope. Then, I put all my findings together: mother alert and conscious, mildly dehydrated, thirty-six-week-sized uterus, adequate liquor, vertex presentation, cervical os 8 cm, foetal heart rate of 150 beats per minute and maternal heart rate of 100 beats per minute. Thank God! My drooping spirits soared high like a hornbill.

'She's going to be all right,' I told the women confidently. She would deliver in two to three hours' time. She needed to rest and have plenty of fluids to quench her thirst.

* * *

It was two o'clock in the morning. The reek of damar smoke had stuffed my nostrils with watery mucus for the past two hours. It was warm inside the room compared to the chilly air outside.

I remembered that a senior colleague of mine, Kak Lathipah, once told me about interesting restrictions during labour according to various cultural beliefs. Thorny vines of *mengkuang* leaves must be curtained along the window and doors. This would scare away banshees that prey on newborns. Freshwater turtles are gravely forbidden to be brought into the room. It would cause the foetal head to move in and out like that of a turtle! A pair of scissors or preferably a betel nut cutter must be kept under the pillow or mat at all times. The weapon was considered effective to deter vampiric entities such as the *penanggal* from harming the woman and the child.

Kak Lathipah and I became close friends the moment the head of obstetrics and gynaecology department assigned her as my mentor one evening. Kak Lathipah was a jovial person. She was a senior nurse and had conducted thousands of deliveries single-handedly at many district clinics and hospitals. Many senior nurses and medical officers sought her guidance. Her experience, as I increasingly noticed then, was more practical, concise and patient-oriented than any guidelines in the nursing or midwifery textbooks that I had read.

'Go out there, Azmir, experience is the best teacher! Do no harm, Azmir, remember. Do no harm first. Do not rush when we conduct any delivery. Always assess the patient and we must prepare for the worst outcomes.' Those were her last words before I was sent to Belaga Community Clinic with another assistant medical officer.

* * *

'Misi, misi!' I was awakened from my reminiscences by a strong pat over the back of my hand. The woman was now in great pain.

I instructed her to breathe properly. Sweat beaded her body as if she had just run through the rain. Her water broke. Clear amniotic fluid oozed through the labia, trailing down, staining the mengkuang mat.

'*Sakit, teran*, sakit, teran . . .' I repeated the words like a mantra. She understood my instructions. The other women cheered, and mopped the perspiration off her body.

Her cervical opening was fully opened. 'Crowning' was seen at the introitus.

'It's already down there. You must relax and push. This won't take long,' I assured her.

Lana opened a small wooden box, about the size of a clenched fist, and took out a metallic blade. She aimed the tip of the blade towards the lower lips of the labia.

'What is that? What are you doing?' I asked Lana, hoping that she did not plan to extend the labial opening—yes, she wanted to cut it. She dragged the blade to take a quick bite on the swollen labia. I hold her hands, to show my disapproval of her decision. Other younger women nodded their heads and agreed with me to not proceed with this unhygienic episiotomy.

'It is not clean and it is not necessary. You need a proper pair of scissors to make one sharp cut, not a blade to carve the flesh. The wound will lead to excessive bleeding!'

Lana pulled a face and embroiled me in a feud. She stood up and tossed the blade into a corner; somehow it ricocheted back towards me. It landed safely a few inches away from me. She then flounced out to the veranda with quelling hauteur, leaving the rest of us gaping at her.

'Push harder! It's coming out!' I cupped my hands around the baby's slimy head, ready to guide the rest of its body to slide out along the pelvic curve. I reached for the baby's neck and twisted it gently to release its shoulder and the rest of the trunk. Finally, the baby slid out from his nine-month confinement.

I clamped a portion of the umbilical cord with my fingers to hold it in place and cut it with a sterile pair of scissors, much to the horror of the women. They protested saying that the placenta would crawl up upwards into the chest.

'You hold the cord and wait for the placenta!' I dismissed their claims. I put the baby on a piece of dry cloth and wiped his body thoroughly. There was an audible gasp as I dried his body. Please cry, please cry! I stroked his back and smacked his bottom, again and again, to stimulate him. Cry! Now! Cry louder! The baby cried out a lusty yell and kicked his four limbs. The response was joyous to the eyes and ears.

* * *

I tracked along the umbilical cord and waited for it to crawl out by itself. The membranes were intact, and the cotyledons were in place. I surrendered the placenta to the ladies and let them proceed to the burial ritual. From there onwards, I had no objections with them. They could do whatever they wanted with the placenta.

I put the full-term baby boy next to the mother. He wriggled like a *sago* worm in the *batik*. I offered her a bowl of clean, boiled water. She took some sips and smiled at me, perhaps thanking me for breaking the rules. I had learnt that her name was Ani.

I saw some women rummaging through the baskets in the room. They demonstrated the traditional way of brewing herbal drinks for *pantang*. The ingredients were mostly leaves, dried nuts, tree barks and roots. Water was boiled in a small metal pot using the indoor firewood stove. The mixture was grounded and scattered into the boiling water. The powdered herbs decolourized the water with a strong reddish hue. It was as red as the blood. The minty steams decongested my nose and warmed my heart.

'Koook! koook! koook!' We heard a distinct thud as we brewed our concoction. Everyone raised their eyebrows and frowned worriedly. We checked the baskets and emptied many containers. We found only clothes and herbal leaves.

'Koook! koook!' the sound mocked us, as if the thing was prancing right under our noses. We turned our clueless heads around, this way and that, inspecting every inch of the room.

'*Siya*! Siya!' Ani pointed at a *tempayan* standing at a corner of the room. The jar contained rainwater. What could possibly be hiding in it?

I approached the jar slowly, with a small parang in my hand, ready to slash anything that jumped at us. The jar had a little water in it. It was light when I shook it. I shoved aside the rattan basket that sealed the mouth of the jar and let it roll to the floor. I peered into the jar and saw that the water was gurgling!

'Something is in there,' I told the women. They trailed behind me holding the oil lamp to enlighten our curiosity.

To our surprise, it was a turtle, clanging the inner wall of the jar with its claws, trying to get out. 'Koook, koook, koook!' A similar sound rang out from the depths of the jar, thus solving the mystery of the night.

'Why there's a turtle in here? This is a freshwater turtle! This is forbidden inside this room, right?' I interrogated the women. The discovery was a bolt from the blue. None of them could explain it. They whispered amongst themselves, soliciting possible reasons behind the event.

'This is why she had difficulty delivering,' I exhorted the taboo back at them. 'Who put this in here?'

The women were astounded. To prevent more catastrophes, I grabbed the turtle and hurled it through the window. 'Ploosh!' The turtle hit the river with a splash.

* * *

The drizzle suddenly abated. A third of the pillars were submerged in the water as the tide set in rigorously. I saw nothing but water encircling the longhouse with its crusading zeal, as if it wanted to swallow us into its throat.

Penghulu Ranang entered the room. The other women hurried out. He sat down beside Ani and kissed the baby. He smiled at me and thanked me with a glistening you-have-done-well glare. At that instant, I realized that Ani was his wife!

Ani, looking slightly more energetic after taking herbal fluids, sat up and spilt the tea. 'I saw Lana put the turtle into the jar. I have been hearing the sounds for days. The other women were too afraid to confront her. They're afraid of her.'

'Really? Why would she do that?' The accusation was an instant eye-opener.

'You must rest and sleep,' Penghulu Ranang interrupted our Q and A session.

Ani blinked rapidly at her husband and before she could open her mouth to explain further, Penghulu laid her on the mat and gave the baby a kiss. Penghulu cued me with a nod. We headed to the indoor veranda to have a more private chat.

It was quiet that morning as the occupants had gone to sleep. A row of flat-wick kerosene lamps were fixed on the wall to embellish the entire stretch of the longhouse, which had about sixty *pintu*. The lamps were antique but extremely useful in a place with no electricity. When I was young, I liked to play with the protruding, toothed knob, adjusting the wick and watching the flame grow and shrink. If the flame grew too big, tarry soot would stain the upper portion of the slender glass chimney.

I followed Penghulu to the other end of the veranda. We sat and leaned against the windowsill. From there, I could see Katibas River disembowel its watery content to flood the adjacent mangrove swamps along this longhouse.

'*Terima kasih*,' Penghulu started the conversation. 'You have saved her and my son.' After a long pause, he continued, 'Ani is my third wife. The second one passed away during childbirth with the baby. Lana is my first one. Lana cannot make a baby any more. I want a child. So, I found another woman, but Lana doesn't like any of them.'

I nodded.

'Lana did give me a son, but he was eaten by a crocodile many years ago,' Penghulu Ranang recalled the tragedy. The cigarette which was rolled like a small cone with the smaller ends stuck between his lips glowed in the darkness.

'*Kesian*,' I offered my condolences. I pitied all of them— Penghulu, Ani, Lana, the crocodile and also, the newborn. I also wanted to pity the pond turtle that I had just flung out of the window.

'You've saved me from the curse. If a man passes away without having a son as his heir, he will turn into a crocodile forever. I don't want to be a crocodile. There are already many crocodiles in the river, and more in Rajang and Belaga.'

I agreed with him. No one wants to become a crocodile or be eaten by the crocodiles, in whatever way.

He finished his cigarette and extinguished the glowing end by stubbing it out on the windowsill.

I spent the night at the longhouse. I slept in a corner of the veranda. Penghulu had gone into the room to accompany Ani and their newborn son. The flood had not reached its maximum height yet, but soon everything would subside. Lying on the newly woven mengkuang mat, I could feel an eerie aura lurking directly beneath my spine.

The next morning, when I gazed out of the window, I saw a lady paddle a small *sampan* out from the longhouse into the river. After studying her gestures and expressions, I recognized Lana. The little boat was laden with many things. She ventured into the river alone without looking back.

The flood had not receded. It drizzled again that morning after an overnight downpour thus increasing the volume of the flood. The longhouse was still surrounded by the muddy water with all sorts of debris floating around.

* * *

Two days later, the flood reluctantly drained back into the river, leaving piles of mud and sand all over the place.

Ani and her baby were well. Breastfeeding had been fully established. While waiting for the perahu, I taught hand-washing techniques to the women and educated them on the need to vaccinate children and practise healthy lifestyles. Penghulu Ranang gave me a tempayan full of rice grains, a basket of *dabai* and a collection of enchanted woodcrafts to protect me from evil spirits.

The salty tang of the air was instantly replaced by an acetous smell of rotting fronds as nipa palms began to appear in unending rows on the banks. Some bore bunches of globular flowers and brownish fruit clusters. An hour later, their ranks thinned out. There, in the bend of the river, we saw an overturned sampan partially buried in the muddy bank.

We anchored our perahu and lifted up the sampan with care. There were many jars, beads, necklaces, utensils, woodworks and boxes with wet clothes piled beneath it.

'Lana!' Penghulu Ranang recognized the belongings.

We screened the area, picking up hints of her potential whereabouts. Everything was probably submerged beneath the mud or into the water in the river. Lana had not been missing for the past two days. Her relatives told us that she had gone to see her parents in Nanga Sebuluh longhouse. The longhouse is a half-day journey by perahu.

'What's going on here?' I demanded. I noticed many scratches and dents over the hull.

'Yes. These are her things,' asserted Penghulu Ranang. His eyes widened and brimmed with tears.

We took her belongings and continued our journey.

'Where could she be?' I wondered.

Not far from the riverbank we saw a float of saltwater crocodiles sunbathing in the mud. As we rowed our perahu passing by them, the biggest crocodile yawned, displaying a set of ferocious fangs.

The Lantern Maker's Wife

Clara Mok

I stood aside and watched Ah Leong whittle down bamboo strips for his handmade lanterns. A splinter pricked his left hand and he winced.

'What the . . . !' he cursed. His eighty-three-year-old face scrunched up like a rag.

I stretched out my hands to soothe his pain, but my formless hand simply glided through his. Ah Leong, I am content sitting next to you, just being near you. How I miss the days when we sat at the hawker centre, knee to knee, watching the world go by as we sipped our soya bean drink.

How I miss those trips to Pek Kio Market. Like children on a scavenger hunt, we crouched by the rubbish dump. The moment cane baskets were discarded by the vegetable seller, we swooped down on them. Our children were puzzled why we grinned like pirates with new-found treasure when we only brought back baskets to fashion into lanterns.

Today is the Mid-Autumn Festival and also our sixtieth wedding anniversary. I cannot miss this day for anything in the world. Ah Leong, I know you cherish this day the most, so I came home specially to be with you.

Ah Leong put down the offending bamboo strips and picked up a floral lantern which was the size of a large beach ball. Its red heart-shaped petals extended outwards in all their glory. His deft hands attached sequins on to the edges of the cellophane flower. He let out a soft sigh, the corners of his mouth crept upwards to signify satisfaction of a craft done well. 'You'd love this, May Lin.'

You're thinking of me. I blushed; my heart was aflutter like the first time we dated. Yes! Yes! Ah Leong, you're right. I love them. Leong, you may think I'm silly, but I want you to feel me, call me by my name; but why can't you hear me?

I flashed past a mirror. Having no reflection jerked me awake to the brutal reality that, in my current form, my loved ones were unable to detect my presence.

I must do something! I must do something!

I floated around in a frenzy before I saw our wedding album and an invitation card wedged within its pages. Not sparing any effort, I pushed the card, causing it to land on the table before Ah Leong. At the same time, the radio crackled with the saccharine voice of Teresa Teng crooning the soulful ballad 'May There Be Eternity of Life':

Sorrows and joy, partings and reunions are part of life.
So is the bright or dim, wax and wane of the moon.
Time is bound to be imperfection.
May we share the beauty of the moon for a long time, even
though we are miles apart.

Ah Leong displayed a flash of recognition on his wrinkled face. 'May Lin!'

Yes! I'm here! I'm here! But he still cannot hear me.

Ah Leong's hand trembled as he gripped the invitation card 'Wedding of Leong Meng Kheng and Wong May Lin'. Some gold letters had flaked off and brown dots punctuated the card. He cast a longing look at it. 'May Lin . . . watch over us . . . our family . . .'

Lisa, my golden-haired granddaughter ran up to Ah Leong.

'*Tai gong*!' Lisa said, shaking Ah Leong's hand. Ah Leong winced as the splinter pricked his skin.

'What is it?' asked Ah Leong.

'Aunt Denise bought a big lantern with disco light!' said Lisa, her arms outstretched to indicate the enormity of the lantern.

'Show me!' he commanded. Lisa tugged at his hand, as he hobbled to the living room.

Sensing an imminent conflict, I used my body to block Ah Leong from view, but he could see right through me.

There, sitting amongst his handcrafted lanterns, was a monstrous variation. The disco ball in the centre shot blue, red and green laser light in clean, robotic lines.

Ah Leong's fists clenched, slowly expelling his breath.

Leong, cool down, will you?

To Ah Leong, buying an electronic lantern was akin to giving a slap to the master craftsman. Worse still, our great grandchildren were dancing to the metallic tune of 'London Bridge is Falling Down'.

'What's all this?' bellowed Ah Leong.

All the children gasped and reached for their mummies and daddies. Ah Leong gripped the electronic lantern, swung

open the panel at the bottom to reveal a clutch of batteries.
He removed them with a flourish and dumped them into a
bin. The irksome song fizzled out and the light dimmed in
an instant.

'Look at this horrible thing. It only looks nice. Without
batteries, it's totally useless.'

Brandon clung on to Denise's sundress, lamenting,
'Mummy, my lantern!'

'Grandpa, you can't do this,' said Denise. 'My kid has to
keep up with the times—'

'Rubbish!' interrupted Ah Leong, his lips quivering.

'For heaven's sake, we do this for you,' Denise argued.

A vein pulsated in Ah Leong's neck and his back stiffened.

Kum Yoke chided, 'Denise, watch your manners.'

Turning to Ah Leong, Kum Yoke pleaded, 'Sorry, father,
it's my fault. I spoiled her. Forgive me, father.'

Ah Leong grunted an acceptance.

Kum Yoke reprimanded Denise, 'Why can't you just give
in to Grandpa? After all, it's only once a year.'

Seemingly possessed, Denise picked up the electronic
lantern by its neon plastic holder. Her eyes glazed over as she
disappeared into the lift.

'Mum, my lantern!' whimpered Brandon.

Some children gasped as they peeped to see Denise
opening the lid of a giant rubbish chute and dumping the
electronic lantern into it. Brandon sobbed and Kum Yoke
distracted him with a toy car.

I release a huge breath of relief as peace reigned in our
family once more.

That's right, Ah Leong, forgive and move on. Do keep the
peace in the family, for my sake.

As I followed Ah Leong down the corridor to the balcony
of our five-room private apartment, he stopped by the familiar

marble table overflowing with offerings and sighed. Ah Leong, as I walk beside you, I cannot help noticing that your hair has taken on more shades of white and the gullies around your eyes have deepened. You look more hunched than before. Hey, I've only been away a year and you've shrivelled.

Billowing smoke from two giant red candles shrouded the sacred moon, lending a mysterious air to its perfect symmetry. The dramatic brilliance of the moon illuminated the festive traditional delights: a gourd-shaped pomelo, *lengkok*, boiled baby taros, traditional mooncakes and snow-skin mooncakes. Auspicious red paper-cuttings were placed on the food.

When I was alive, I had laid out blushers and lipsticks in neat rows as offerings for the goddess of the moon so that the ladies in my family would be as beautiful as Chang Er. I also made sure that my great-grandchildren received blessings for their studies by placing an array of schoolbags, pens and notebooks on the table of offerings. These traditions had been passed down from my grandparents to my parents. For years, I held fast to them. I dabbed my tears when I saw my children had laid similar offerings.

My great-grandchildren gaped in fascination when I told them mooncakes concealing slips of paper with the revolt date led to the successful uprising by Zhu Yuanzhang, ending the Yuan dynasty and starting the Ming dynasty. Much to my amusement, they looked into their mooncakes for such messages too.

I wondered if they remembered the more tragic version where Chang Er's husband, Houyi, shot down nine of the ten suns and was awarded an elixir of immortality. The moon goddess, Chang Er swallowed the elixir to prevent it from falling into evil hands. As a result, her body became weightless and she floated to the moon with a rabbit in tow, forever separated from Houyi. They asked me why she brought along a rabbit and not a dog or a cat. I told them the story of a father and a mother rabbit wanting to soothe Chang Er, not wanting her to feel lonely and sent one of their four children to her for company. I wondered if my family would do the same if they knew I was lonely.

From the dining room, I watched Kum Yoke. A wisp of hair falling over her forehead, she wore a smile on her ruddy face as she pottered about in the kitchen. Kum Yoon, Kum Wah and Kum Mei were serving the dishes. Kum Seng was lounging on the sofa, reading newspapers, while his brothers-in-law discussed the latest Toto million-dollar draw. My lovely children, how I miss you! I will come and visit you on this day every year.

Ah Leong, I'll never forget the time Kum Seng was born. What a cheerful baby he was! I remember your mum's sternness melting away. She was so pleased to have a boy carry the Leong surname that she gave him an extra red packet for good luck.

Next came our second child, Kum Leng. Pity she was born of a weak constitution at war time. She did not survive her teens, succumbing to pneumonia. I cried until there were no more tears in me.

Our eldest surviving daughter, Kum Yoke, brought us joy. With Kum Seng being the male heir, your mother tolerated having two girls, but her patience wore thin when I gave birth to Kum Yoon, Kum Wah and Kum Mei. I remember her snatching the babies from the midwife, prying open the swaddling cloth wrapping the newborn just to have a look at the baby's genitals. Each time, her shoulder would sag when she realized that our family had to raise another granddaughter.

'A waste of money, the bunch of them!' your mother complained. 'After all, when they get married, they are like water splashed out of the house.'

Our girls brought such joy to the family. When I walked down the street, neighbours would point me out, 'That's the woman who gave birth to five girls!'

* * *

As Ah Leong made his way from the balcony to the dining room, I sat beside him at the head of the table. Smile, Ah Leong, smile. Why are you looking so sullen?

Three pairs of innocent eyes stared up at me.

I covered my eyes with my hands and revealed them again. It was a gesture I had used before and one that the children were familiar with. Shrieks of laughter pierced the air as they scrambled for hiding places. Seven-year-old Brandon peeked out from under the dining table.

'What are you doing, Brandon?' asked Kum Yoke.

'Nothing, grandma. We're playing with *tai por*.' But Kum Yoke was already heading back into the kitchen.

Chopsticks and soup spoons clattered on the table as the children scrambled to be the first to land their posteriors on stools.

I waved my hands vigorously. Stop shaking or you'll spill the soup. Behave!

Wanting to please me, my great-grandchildren sat still like statues. On this special day, I was relieved that my great-grandchildren could sense me and wanted so much to please me.

Kum Yoke marched into the room. 'You kids had better—' she stopped mid-sentence and scratched her head, mumbling, 'Funny, I thought I heard noises earlier.'

The children's eyes twinkled as they stifled their giggles.

'Dinner's ready!' Kum Yoke called out and the adults shuffled to the table.

Thirty members of the Leong family sat elbow-to-elbow around two elongated oval dinner tables piled with Cantonese dishes—stir-fried sweet-and-sour pork with pineapple, pan-fried prawns, *choy sum* in oyster sauce, and steamed fish in soya sauce garnished with spring onion, cilantro, ginger and chilli strips.

I rubbed my hands with glee as my favourite dish was served—braised sea-cucumber with mushrooms. I recalled how Ah Leong worked hard as an accountant in a small trading firm to raise the family. Slowly, we were able to afford adding pork belly, then sea cucumbers to the dish.

'I prepared this dish specially for Mah.'

To prove my presence, I sent a gust of wind blowing against the curtains.

'Mah! Is that you?' Kum Yoke asked, blinking away tears.

'Possibly,' replied Kum Seng. 'She misses us too.'

'Come on, your Mah won't like it. She always said "food is best eaten hot". Eat! Eat!' Ah Leong said.

You understand me best, Ah Leong. Dry your tears, Kum Yoke.

Taking his cue, everyone began pushing rice grains into their mouths with the tips of their chopsticks. Watercress soup simmering over a slow fire, its bubbling broth of pork ribs reminded me of home. Dinner continued with the usual cacophony of voices, jostling, jokes and camaraderie. Denise placed food on Ah Leong's plate and he accepted with grace. Lisa was seated two seats away from Ah Leong and chatted to him about how the elephant cellophane lantern Ah Leong made amazed everyone.

'Do you know why lanterns are so special?' Ah Leong asked Lisa.

'Lanterns make us happy and bring us together!' Lisa replied.

'So clever. Who taught you that?'

'Tai gong! My friends' lanterns are dumb. They keep repeating the same music!'

'Tai gong's lanterns are the best, right?'

'Yes!' Lisa said, giving the thumbs up.

I could not suppress my joy to see Ah Leong opening up to our loved ones in my absence. Somehow, I felt alive again, being in the midst of my children, grandchildren and great-grandchildren. My family is together again.

We sipped Chinese tea and savoured mooncakes while admiring the incandescent moon. Great-grandchildren played in the open space downstairs under the watchful eye of Kum Yoke. Every year, Ah Leong would create new designs for his great-grandchildren. This year's additions were the panda lanterns, Jia Jia and Kai Kai, the panda duo gifted to Singapore by China. After that, all of us went downstairs together and placed thirty lanterns in two neat rows. Lighting the candles proved to be a humongous task.

'Light mine first!'

'No, mine first!'

'Hey!'

The great-grandchildren jostled one another, except Brandon. His face was glum.

Line up in one row—the youngest in front! I raised both arms and left them there, waiting. The children froze for a moment before getting in line. Then I dropped my arms.

'Wow, this is the only time of the year when you kids behave so well!' Kum Yoke remarked.

Brandon, do you want to join them? He shook his head. Come, let's play with the sand then. His eyes twinkled and he headed for the sandpit.

Finally, all thirty lanterns sparkled in a rainbow of lights.

'Tai gong, your lanterns are so beautiful!' exclaimed Lisa as she savoured the sight in front of her, her head swivelling left to right and back.

'Here's yours,' offered Ah Leong.

Lisa's hands shook with excitement as she clasped the wooden stick with the Angry Bird lantern tightly in her hands. However, the lantern swung from side to side like a pendulum and the candle flame was extinguished, leaving a wispy trail of smoke.

'My lantern!' Lisa howled.

Ah Leong clasped his reassuring hand over her tiny hands. Soon, the swinging momentum of the lantern slowed to a halt. Ah Leong winked as he said, 'You're a big girl. Hold it still, okay?'

Lisa nodded.

Ah Leong let go of his hands. To secure the lantern, Ah Leong used a pair of pliers to tighten the wire frame of the candle holder so that the candle would fit snugly. Then he struck a match, its flame igniting the candle wick. Lisa beamed when her lantern was flickering once again.

'Tai gong, you're so clever!' Lisa said. The lantern's flame danced in her pupils.

I struck the jackpot when I caught Ah Leong smiling for the first time that evening. To him, his cellophane lanterns were perfect in every way. For the Angry Bird lantern, he made two red feathers on its head snipped from an old cardboard box. To complete its iconic eyebrows, he cut out two pieces of rectangular black cardboard and made them tilt inwards to a shape of the letter V. For the beak, he cut a triangular shape from yellow cardboard.

Only I could tell that some parts of Ah Leong's handmade bamboo lanterns had cellophane paper sticking out at the corners, not visible to the untrained eye. Others needed patching up due to rough handling. Yet every lantern in itself was an exclusive piece of traditional art, unique to the Chinese heritage and he was eager to pass on this artform to his descendants.

I focused on the flame of the candle dancing with abandon. So vibrant! Memories of my wedding anniversaries stayed vivid as the images of Ah Leong's handmade lanterns floated into my mind—a peony, a lotus, a hibiscus, an orchid, a rabbit (the zodiac year I was born), a swallow, a carp and even a phoenix! My favourites were the floral lanterns Ah Leong made for me in the first few years of our marriage.

Against the pitch dark of the night, thirty, brightly lit, handmade lanterns cast elongated dancing shadows on the asphalt. The lanterns' brilliance erupted in a kaleidoscope of colours—red, blue, green and orange—each trying to outshine the other. The glow of lanterns illuminated the exuberant faces of my great-grandchildren, evoking a sense of nostalgia as I was enveloped in familial love. How I love these lantern walks!

Illuminated by the splendour of the full moon, the entire family contingent trooped to the neighbourhood playground. The children handed their lanterns to their parents before sticking candles in the sand. Kum Yoke and her sisters lit up the candles. The flickering candles were arranged in a gigantic heart shape, symbolizing love and unity. I watched my family huddle close. Some squatted in front, others bent forward to avoid blocking the rest.

'Come join us!' the children beckoned to me.

The adults looked around to see who the children were calling. Brandon, kicking sand in a distance, ran towards them and the adults returned to posing for a family photograph.

My heart was in shreds as I stood next to Ah Leong, knowing that the family photograph would never bear my image.

'Hey! I'm first!'

'No, it's me!'

After the lantern walk, the children shoved one another, scrambling to be the first to enter the apartment.

Where are your manners? Let Tai gong enter first!

The children stopped dead and stepped aside to let Ah Leong pass.

'Thank you,' said Ah Leong.

Behind him, the children kept straight faces but started jostling one another.

Stop it, children! Blow out the candles and take off your shoes before you enter the house. One at a time! I beamed with pride when my great-grandchildren followed my instructions.

'Tai gong, I want to learn to make lanterns!' said Lisa.

'Me too!' said Brandon.

Ah Leong prepared one set of materials for each child to create a simple lantern. He also helped them to twist the bamboo strips. Parents joined in the session to bask in the family bonding and joy. The great-grandchildren held their self-made lanterns in their hands and chorused, 'We can't wait to light our own lanterns!'

Ah Leong nodded his head, his countenance glowing.

At the balcony, I joined Kum Yoke and her sisters as they lit up the incense sticks and prayed to the moon goddess for good health, safety and happiness. When the ceremony ended, they apportioned the offerings to be shared by family members. Lisa fell asleep the moment she plonked herself on the sofa, her hand clutching her lantern and had to be carried to the car by her parents. One by one, family members waved and left. Goodbye my dears. See you next year. I'm starting to miss all of you! I felt a dull ache in my chest and a lump in my throat.

I watched Ah Leong caress the floral lantern before him, basking in its iridescent glow of red and yellow, conveying an enchanting aura to the room. The flickering ring cast lively moving images on the ceiling.

I ran a finger along the edge of his shirt collar. Ah Leong, I miss being by your side every day, cooking for you, fussing over you and strolling after dinner. I miss the simple pleasures of drinking the soya bean drink and eating carrot cake at the hawker centre with you. I miss watching the drama serials together. I miss pottering around the plants with you on the balcony. I miss your lovely lanterns most of all.

I summoned my power and the radio roared to life Teresa. Teng's voice rang out once more.

May we share the beauty of the moon for a long time, even though we are miles apart.

Ah Leong, heaven and earth may separate us, but our hearts would forever be linked as one. I will wait patiently for the day when you come and join me.

Glossary

A-levels	A British pre-university examination.
Abah	Malay term of address for father.
adab	Malay word for manners and expected conduct.
Alhamdulillah	Arabic word which means 'praise be to God'.
amal jariah	Malay term for charity in the service of society.
Amma / Mah	Terms of address for mother.
anyeng-anyengan	Javanese word for discomfort when urinating.
Apa	Literally means 'what?' in Sarawakian Malay; can also mean 'any problem?'.

Assalamualaikum	A traditional Muslim greeting in the Arabic language to mean 'peace to you'.
ba	A Filipino expression, usually at the end of a sentence.
Babu	A respectful title or form of address for a man, especially an educated one.
bahu	Hindi word for daughter-in-law.
baithak	Hindi word for a sitting room.
baju kebaya	Traditional blouse that is usually worn, with a matching batik sarong, by women in Southeast Asia of Javanese, Malay, and the Malacca Peranakan descent.
Balik India	Malay phrase for 'Go back to India'.
Bao Sheng Da Di	A Chinese deity who is worshipped as the god of medicine. The Baosheng Cultural Festival in Taiwan is a two-month-long celebration of the birthday of the deity in the third lunar month.
barong	A type of Filipino clothes/shirt worn by Tagalogs.
Bas	Hindi word for enough.

batik	A fabric made with wax-resistant dye, commonly found in Southeast Asia.
beta ji	Hindi term to address a child.
bhajans	Devotional hymns sung by Hindus, Jains and Sikhs.
Bodoh	Malay word for stupid.
Boyak	Crocodile in Malay, Iban or other indigenous tribe language.
chacha	Hindi term of address for uncle.
chopped	Singapore slang for stamping a date on a book.
choy sum	Cantonese name for a green leafy vegetable characterized by distinct yellow flowers; it is translated to Chinese to mean 'heart of the vegetable' or *cai xin*.
Chup	Hindi word which means 'shut up'.
Cik	Malay word for Miss.
Cikgu	A term of address in Malay for teacher.
dabai (Canarium odontophyllum)	An indigenous seasonal fruit which grows naturally in the wild and can only be found in Borneo Island, especially Sarawak. It is commonly known as 'Sarawak olive' due to its resemblance to olives.

dangdutan	A genre of folk music popular throughout Indonesia and the Malay world incorporating elements of Hindustani, Arabic, Malay, and local music, that is often but not always associated with sexually suggestive female singers and dancers.
desh	Hindi word for home in the plains.
dey / dei	A Tamil term of address said in anger or affection to address a man or boy or amongst male friends.
diyas	A small cup-shaped oil lamp made of baked clay.
Encik	Malay word for mister/Mr.
ghagras	A traditional clothing of women from the Indian subcontinent.
gobi ka paratha	A North Indian paratha that is stuffed with flavoured grated cauliflower and other vegetables.
Harijans	Members of a hereditary Hindu group of the lowest social and ritual status.
horning	In Singapore English, the word 'horn' is sometimes used as a verb.
ikan bilis	Malay term for small, dried anchovies.
Itulah	Malay word for 'that's it'.

jaipongan	A popular traditional Sundanese (West Javanese) style of music and dance entertainment incorporating martial arts and sexually suggestive movements.
jie jie	Hokkien/Mandarin term of address for elder sister.
kakar	Hindi word for a barking deer / Indian muntjac.
Kawan	Malay word for friend.
ke	A word added at the end of a question for emphasis.
keling	A derogatory and offensive Malay word for Malaysians of South Indian origins.
Kenak	Literally means 'why?' in Sarawakian Malay; can also mean 'what's wrong?' or 'why not?'.
kerongsang	A type of brooch that is used to pin together the *baju kebaya* at the front.
Kesian	To mean 'I feel sorry for (someone)' in Sarawakian Malay.
khichdi	A South Asian dish made of rice and lentil.
Klingons	A fictional race of aliens from the original *Star Trek* series.
kor kor	Hokkien term of address for elder brother.

kuniang	Mandarin word for girl or young woman.
kway teow	Hokkien term for flat rice noodles.
lah	Malay suffix or tag that softens the tone of the word or sentence.
lalapan	Indonesian word for the fresh vegetables and herbs that can accompany rice.
lengkok	Cantonese word for water caltrop, which is in the shape of a small bat with outstretched wings. After steaming it, break open the hard outer covering and a fruit (similar to a nut) can be eaten.
lompat dulu	'Jump first' in Sarawakian Malay.
mabuk	Malay word for drunk.
macha	An affectionate term of address for bro or dude, among young people, although the original meaning of the word is brother-in-law in the Tamil language.
Maadher-chod	An obscene and ancient expression of anger in Hindi.
mau jumpa	'I want to see you now' in Sarawakian Malay.
memsaab	Hindi term for madam.

mengkuang	Screw pine leaves.
Misi	A colloquial term in Malay, possibly from the English word 'missy', referring to nurses.
MLM	Multi-level marketing.
moi	French word for 'me', used humorously in English to denote affected surprise.
monyet	Malay word for monkey.
Munna	An affectionate term of address in Hindi for son.
munthani	Tamil word for the end of a saree which is draped over the shoulder.
NBI	National Bureau of Investigation; some employers require prospective employees to get clearances from the said agency to check if they have criminal records.
ombothu	Tamil derogatory word for effeminate boys/men.
pantang	Malay word for postpartum.
pardes	Hindi word for foreign country.
pariah	A slur, referring to an untouchable.
pasar malam	Malay term for night market.
pedas	An Indian milk-based sweetmeat.

penanggal	A nocturnal vampiric entity from Malay ghost myths, often attacks women in labour.
Penghulu	The headman or chief of a region in traditional Indonesian, Bornean and Malay society.
perahu	Malay word for a small sailing vessel commonly used in Southeast Asia.
pintu	A unit referring to an individual room in the longhouse or 'doors' in Iban language.
pondan	Malay derogatory word for effeminate boys/men.
potteh	Tamil derogatory word for effeminate boys/men.
pottus	Tamil word for coloured dots on the forehead, between the eyebrows of Hindu women.
pradakshna	A term used in Hinduism and Buddhism for the ritual of circumambulation in a clockwise direction around a shrine, image, sacred object or even a town.
rezeki	Malay word for sustenance as decided by God.
rogan josh	A meat dish of Kashmiri origin.
sago	A palm weevil larva.
saabji	Hindi term for sir.

Saenah . . . nya sae nya ngenah . . .	To mean 'good and delicious' in a local dialect in Indonesia.
Sakit, teran	To mean 'if you feel pain, please push' in Sarawakian Malay.
sampan	Malay word for a relatively flat-bottomed smaller sailing vessel than a *perahu*.
sayang	Malay word to address a loved one.
sel rotis	A traditional, sweet, ring-shaped, Nepali rice bread/doughnut.
shanti path	Literally means 'path to peace' or 'peace road' in Hindi; refers to prayers for the departed and funeral wake.
shee-shee	A child's word for urinating or urine. It mimics the whistling sound adults sometimes make to get their toddlers to urinate.
Siya	Sarawakian Malay word for 'there'.
STPM	Short for Sijil Tinggi Persekolahan Malaysia, a pre-university examination in Malaysia.
Surah Ya Sin	A chapter in the Quran.
tahlilan	The Islamic ritual of reciting praise and praying for the deceased and their family after death.
Tai gong	Cantonese and Mandarin term to address great-grandfather.

tai por	Cantonese and Mandarin term to address great-grandmother.
tarik	Literally means 'to pull' in Malay; to pour repeatedly between two cups, leaving drink frothy.
tempayan	A wide-mouthed earthenware jar commonly found in Southeast Asia.
terima kasih	Malay expression which literally means 'accepted with love', to express thanks.
thanggachi	Tamil term of address for younger sister.
TNB	Tenaga Nasional Berhad, Peninsular Malaysia's electric utility company.
Toto	A legalized form of lottery sold in Singapore.
Tung-twa	Fokkien word for growing, hitting puberty.
two stones	These stones are moon blocks (*jiaobei*) made of bamboo roots and are used as divination tools to answer a yes-and-no question.
Waalaikumsalam / Waalaikumussalam	A traditional Muslim greeting in the Arabic language to mean 'peace be upon you' and is said in reply to '*Assalamualaikum*'.

Waghoba	An ancient leopard/tiger deity worshipped by a number of ethnic groups in India. Waghoba has a long history of cooperation with big cats in India, and the knowledge and practices learned from Waghoba in modern times have been invaluable in big cat conservation in India.
Wah-pay-lo	Fokkien Chinese expression akin to 'oh my goodness'.
wakil rakyat	Malay term for a state assembly person or member of parliament.
wan tan mee	A noodle dish of Cantonese origin, with roasted meat and dumplings.
warahmatullahi wabarakatuh	Arabic phrase which means 'God's mercy and blessings'.
yellow triangle	A talisman, which is a long piece of yellow paper with black text folded into a triangle, believed to possess magical properties.
Yen taw	Fokkien phrase for handsome.
zhup lak lao	Hokkien phrase that means 'sixteen storeys'.